PARP 2022

From The TSL PTA

Marigold
ST★R

ELISE PRIMAVERA

Marigold STAR

HARPER

An Imprint of HarperCollinsPublishers

Library of Congress Control Number: 2018965672
ISBN 978-0-06-056951-8

Typography by Molly Fehr
20 21 22 23 24 PC/BRR 10 9 8 7 6 5 4 3 2 1
❖
First paperback edition, 2020

To Maggie Maple—
May you have friends
wherever you go.

WHAT IS YOUR
MAGIC POWER?

1

PROBLEMS IN BRAMBLYCRUMBLY

Marigold had a star above her head.

That's right, a *real*, honest-to-goodness star.

Her parents were delighted. "It's a sure sign that Marigold is marked for greatness!" they often said. Everyone in the entire town of Bramblycrumbly thought so too.

Marigold walked slower than usual down the path with her pet dragon, Lightning. He had watched her practice the Flying Spell all morning till she had finally given up. "I'm not great at anything," she said with a sigh.

"You're great at making friends," Lightning said helpfully. This was true. Everyone liked Marigold Star—even the goblins and the trolls who didn't like anybody.

Marigold's sky-blue dress was covered in grass stains.

Her pink leggings were ripped at both knees. Even the normally bright orange petals on her head had lost their luster and seemed to have wilted. She kicked a pebble out of the way. "It's easy to make friends."

"Not for everybody," Lightning replied.

"It's easier than flying," she muttered. Marigold wished that Lightning could say something to make her feel better, but she had to admit it didn't seem likely she would ever learn to fly. She couldn't even blame the dragon when he said, "You've got a problem."

She *did* have a problem—there was no denying it any longer. Everybody her age was flying by now—except for her. A spotted owl landed on her shoulder. "Hello, Mrs. Moon," Marigold said. "I've got a problem!"

"Nonsense!" The owl flapped to a low branch. "That star over your head is a sure sign—"

"Of greatness. I know all that, Mrs. Moon," Marigold said impatiently. "But I've still got a problem—watch." Marigold crouched as low as she could to get plenty of spring like she'd been taught, flung her arms in the air, and just before she leaped, said the spell. "Spoket! Spoket! Magic poket! Fly!"

Lightning winced. It was always the same whenever Marigold tried this.

Thud! She landed in the dirt.

"OH!" Marigold shouted in exasperation. "What am I doing wrong?"

The owl was an expert on flying and knew exactly what Marigold was doing wrong. "It's simple. You need to leap with a sense of conviction, Marigold."

"Conviction?" Marigold had no idea what that meant.

"Confidence!" Mrs. Moon exclaimed. "Like you are sure you will fly—like you're not afraid!"

Marigold scrunched up her nose. "But I *am* afraid."

"*That's* your problem!" the owl said, and flew away.

Marigold got up slowly and dusted herself off. "Now I have two problems, Lightning. What am I going to do?"

The dragon stared. "Um, Marigold? Your . . . star . . ."

"What about my star?" Marigold raised her eyes and gasped. Her star, which had glowed for as long as she could remember—every day and night of her entire life—was blinking.

Off. On. Off. On. Off. On. Off. On. Off. On. Off. On.

Lightning couldn't take his eyes from it.

Marigold was scared even to move. "What do you think it means?" she whispered.

The dragon whispered back, "I have no idea."

"Now I have three problems!" Marigold cried.

"This isn't good," Lightning said with dismay. A chilled wind blew, and the dragon shivered. "We should go home. Aren't you supposed to be practicing the Invisibility Spell right now, anyway?"

"Yes, but I don't want to go home, remember?" Marigold replied.

"Oh yeah, that's right—Petal," Lightning said knowingly. "It's just not the same at home anymore, is it?"

"It's not, and that's a problem." Ever since Marigold's new baby sister had arrived, things had changed. Marigold sat down hard on a lumpy log with her chin in her hands. "Now I have four problems!"

"Look on the bright side. . . ." Lightning hesitated.

Marigold knew that her dragon always liked to look on the bright side, but in this case, he was having trouble finding it. He'd probably never known anyone with four problems.

"What are you going to do?" he finally said.

Marigold shook her head. She felt awful, and even though she had Lightning, she looked around for another friend to tell her problems to.

Just then, Bob the Woodcutter's Son came around the corner. He waved the green hat with the four-leaf clover in it that he always wore and called to her. "Hi, Marigold! Want to help me gather wood in the forest?"

It was a chore Bob had to do all the time, so Marigold tried to help whenever she could. But not today. "I can't, Bob."

"Marigold has four problems," Lightning explained.

Bob gazed at the spot over her head. "Your star is blinking."

"And it won't stop," Marigold said. "That's only one of my problems."

"I know how you feel, Marigold," Bob said.

"You do?" Marigold was surprised because Bob never seemed to have any problems.

Bob nodded. "Everyone calls me Bob the Woodcutter's Son, but no one knows if my name is Bob or if I'm the son of a man named Bob the Woodcutter!"

Marigold and Lightning exchanged perplexed glances.

"You see?" the boy exclaimed.

"So, what *is* your name?" Marigold asked, thinking all this time she'd had it wrong.

He waved his hand and smiled. "It's Bob."

"And the Woodcutter?" Lightning asked.

"He's Johann," Bob answered. "So that's my problem, but what are yours, Marigold?"

Lightning ticked them off one by one. "She's marked for greatness, but she can't even fly because she's afraid, and we really should go home but she doesn't want to go home—"

"Petal!" Bob exclaimed. "But why do you need to go home right now?"

Marigold lowered her eyes. "Because I'm supposed to be practicing the Invisibility Spell."

"Wait." Bob pulled his magic wand from a back pocket, stood on one leg, rubbed his stomach in a circular motion with one hand, tapped his head with the wand in his other hand, crossed his eyes, and said, "Magic wand, make me invisible." *Poof!* He disappeared. "You don't know the Invisibility Spell yet?" came Bob's voice, although he was nowhere to be seen.

"I know the spell." Marigold lowered her eyes and bit her

lip. "It's just that it never works when I do it." She reached for her wand to show Bob what she meant, and that's when she realized she'd left it at home. "At least I *think* I left it at home," she said. "Or maybe I put it down while I was talking to Mrs. Moon. . . ." But she didn't remember doing that either. "Oh! I'm always misplacing the silly thing!" She turned to her dragon for help. "Lightning, did you see it?"

"It's right here." Lightning produced the wand—it had become one of his jobs to keep track of it for Marigold.

"You know, Marigold," Bob said—and even though he was still invisible, Marigold could hear the concern in his voice—"I've heard bad things can happen if you lose your magic wand and it gets into the wrong hands."

Marigold's face grew hot with embarrassment. She couldn't even hold on to her own magic wand without losing it. "I've heard that too," she mumbled. "It seems like I'm always losing my wand. You don't think that's another problem, do you?"

"Don't worry, Marigold," Bob said more cheerfully. "You'll always have Lightning to look after it for you."

"That's true," Marigold replied. But Bob hadn't made her feel any better because she still couldn't get the Invisibility

Spell to work right—and it was the easiest spell of all to do. "How will I ever be a fairy god-doctor like my mom or a weather wizard like my dad if I don't even know the Invisibility Spell?"

Bob materialized. "Now that's a problem," he admitted.

Marigold had never been so upset. "I have *five* problems! What am I going to do?"

"I'll help you with the spell, Marigold," Bob offered.

"You will?" Marigold brightened. "Thanks, Bob!"

"But it won't solve your other problems," Lightning reminded.

"Lightning's right. Maybe you should talk to Baddie Longlegs instead," Bob suggested.

"The good troll." Marigold knew him well.

"It's not easy being a troll," Bob said. "He probably has lots of problems!"

"I hope not," Marigold said. Baddie was one of her best friends, and she hated to think that he had lots of problems. Still, maybe Baddie could help—it was worth a try. Marigold and Lightning waved goodbye to Bob and set out to see Baddie Longlegs.

As soon as they were in sight of the bridge, Baddie

Longlegs came running out of his shack to meet them. He was nice looking for a troll, which probably wasn't saying much because he had the standard enormous nose and ears, but he had lovely, long, wavy green hair and dazzling emerald-green eyes. He also kept himself trim—unlike the other trolls who just lay around letting themselves go to pot. Plus, he was an expert knitter and had made himself a jaunty striped scarf that he'd knotted around his neck.

He waved them inside, where brightly colored balls of yarn were stuffed into the many cubbyholes that lined the walls. Everywhere you looked, wicker baskets overflowed with skeins of yarn. Cherry reds to rosy pinks, lemony yellows to burnt oranges, sea greens to rich purple blues— they were all arranged by color. Marigold always loved to see Baddie's latest creations. He knitted socks, sweaters, and scarves on Sunday, mittens and hats on Monday, and the rest of the week he made things for his shack. Everything from the tea cozy over the kettle to the curtains at the window had been knitted by Baddie.

"I'm sorry." Marigold showed him her empty pockets. She visited the troll once a week and always brought him a ball of yarn for his collection—but not today.

He laughed it off. "I don't care about that—I'm always happy to see you, Marigold!" He offered her a seat while Lightning curled up on the checkered, knitted rug beside her. Then the troll settled into his favorite armchair with the carrot-orange knitted slipcovers.

Marigold knew Baddie wanted to talk, but she was too distracted to say anything. The star had never behaved this way before. Was it going to stop blinking? Was it going to disappear? What was it going to do? It was annoying and worrisome at the same time.

Baddie leaned over his knitting basket to pick up a long scarf he'd been working on. Even when he had company, he liked to keep his hands busy. For a while all Marigold could hear was the click, click, clicking sounds of his knitting needles, until he finally commented, "If you don't mind my saying, Marigold—and don't take this the wrong way—but you seem a bit . . . off . . . somehow."

If she raised her eyes as far as they'd go, she could see the light from the annoying blinking star. She muttered, "Off? How?"

"Let's just say you're not altogether yourself," the troll replied.

Marigold pried her attention from the pesky star. "I'm *not* altogether myself," she admitted. "I have five problems, Baddie—*five!*" She explained them all and sighed. "It's just not the same at home anymore either. Right, Lightning?"

"It's definitely not the same," Lightning agreed.

"But on the plus side . . ." Baddie paused to fix a dropped stich. "At least you don't have eleven brothers and sisters to contend with."

"You had that many growing up?" Marigold said, surprised.

"Yes, and they were always hiding my knitting needles and switching my balls of yarn for rotten goblins' eggs."

"That's awful, Baddie!" Marigold felt terrible for her friend, who was always so kind. Now she knew why he lived alone. But it made her wonder what it would have been like if she'd been born a troll like Baddie, growing up in a crowded shack under a bridge with almost a dozen troll brothers and sisters who teased her all the time. Marigold wondered if she would still be as nice as Baddie or if she would be cross like most of the other trolls and never want to share or be friendly.

"Oh, I know I shouldn't complain," Marigold said. "It's

just that my baby sister gets all the attention—if I lived in the forest with Lightning and never went home, my parents wouldn't even notice." Marigold suddenly got an idea. "I know! You could help me build a shack. We could be neighbors, and I could keep you company!"

Baddie was excited. "And I could knit you some curtains and rugs and blankets and slippers and whatever you needed."

"But it still wouldn't solve all your problems," Lightning pointed out. "Like your star."

Marigold raised her eyes and frowned. It was still blinking. "What am I going to do?"

"Maybe you should go see Granny Cabbage?" Baddie said.

"What a good idea!" Marigold's spirits rose. The cabbage lady was one of her best friends.

"It's a long way to Granny's, but maybe you'll get lucky and catch a train," the troll added. "If she can't solve your problems, no one can."

Before she left, Marigold asked him shyly, "Have you ever had five problems, Baddie?"

"The most I've ever had is one." Baddie looked down. He

didn't say anything for so long that Marigold thought he might not tell her at all, when he finally said softly, "My only problem is . . . I'm lonely."

Marigold gently touched the sleeve of his cable-knit sweater. "You shouldn't ever be lonely, Baddie. You're such a good friend, and you're a great knitter too—the best in all of Bramblycrumbly."

The troll smiled because he loved to be complimented on his knitting.

Marigold thanked him for the advice. As she set off for Granny Cabbage's cottage, she wished that she could find a way to help Baddie solve his one problem.

2

SPOOKETY FOREST

The only way to Granny's little cottage was on the other side of a deep, dark wood called Spookety Forest, which was named after a family of ghosts who had lived there for as long as anyone remembered. Spookety Forest was a gloomy place filled with strange creatures. Marigold was always careful because you never knew who (or what) you would meet there, but she also felt protected because she was best friends with the Spooketys and their kids, the ghost children, who flew through the woods all the time.

Marigold and Lightning hurried over Baddie's bridge. On the other side was a wrought iron gate. With a push the gate creaked open eerily. They entered a twilight world of brambles and moss along a path that led under a canopy of trees into Spookety Forest. If you walked, it could take hours to get to Granny's. Of course, Marigold could have hopped onto Lightning's back and they could have flown—her parents had gotten the dragon for this very purpose, to help their daughter get around—but Lightning was slow, and for the most part it was quicker just to walk.

"Do you think a train will come?" Marigold asked.

Lightning shrugged. "Who knows?" He was right. The Spookety family ran the only public transportation system in all of Bramblycrumbly, and it was completely unpredictable. There was no schedule for the ghost train (as it had come to be called), and only the Spooketys could make it rise out of the mist. But if you were lucky and caught one, it was the fastest way to get anywhere in the land.

"Maybe we should call Big Flying Bird?" Marigold suggested.

Lightning grimaced. "Remember the last time we called him and he got mad and left us in the swamp?"

Marigold did remember. It had taken forever to get home, and her boots had never been the same. "At least he could get us to Granny's faster than walking."

Lightning talked right over her. "All I said was that he

was as big as an elephant—which he is. . . ."

Marigold huffed, "You know how sensitive he is about his size, Lightning. Say the spell."

"I don't want to say the spell," Lightning replied peevishly. "*You* say the spell."

"You know when *I* say the spell it never works, and besides, *you're* the one who made him mad in the first place, and—"

"All right, I'll say the spell!" Lightning waved his hands and recited so quickly Marigold could barely understand the words. "Twinkle, twinkle, Big Flying Bird. Come to me with these few words. I wish I may, I wish I might, have the bird I wish tonight!"

Bop! Pop! Shroosh!

Before them stood a magnificent bird. He had long golden legs and a pointy beak. He had lovely black and white feathers and a majestic plume on top of his head. He was as big as an elephant.

The bird gave Lightning a stony stare. "You again!"

"Can you take us to Granny Cabbage's, please?" Lightning asked in his most polite voice.

The bird pointedly ignored the dragon. He folded his

wings in front of his chest like a person would fold their arms and stared at Marigold. "What's with the blinking star?"

"It started today—that's why we need to go see Granny," Marigold said desperately.

"I'm very sensitive to light, and that thing is giving me a headache." The bird narrowed his eyes at the dragon. "Plus, I think I might be too *big* to take you to Granny Cabbage's. Birds aren't supposed to be as big as *elephants*—at least that's what someone told me. . . . Hmmm . . . who would it have been?" The bird looked all around and then glared at Lightning. "Oh, that's right. It was *you*!"

Marigold tried to calm the bird. "Lightning didn't mean anything by it, Big Flying Bird."

"You just called me big!" the bird complained.

"I didn't mean that." Marigold waved her hands as if to erase what she'd just said. "You're just a bird—a *flying* bird. I think—I mean, we both think—you're just the right size!"

Lightning said urgently, "Yes, parrot-size—just like all your brothers and sisters!"

"My brothers and sisters, huh?" The bird nodded as if he were agreeing, but his face told a different story.

Lightning smiled pleasantly in an effort to assume an expression of utter honesty. "Yes, I mean, you're practically as small as they are."

"Yes, practically!" Marigold beamed.

"You're only just a teeny, tiny bit bigger," Lightning added.

"Lightning!" Marigold was horrified. "Don't say the word 'bigger' to him," she whispered.

"*Bigger*?" the bird repeated, and his cheeks, where there were less feathers, became an angry red.

Lightning's smile faded. "So, what do you say, hmmm?"

"Three words," the bird snapped. "Take. The. Train."

Shroosh! Pop! Bop!

The bird vanished.

"Wait! Don't go!" Marigold called but to no avail.

Lightning stood with his hands on his hips, staring at the air where once there was a Big Flying Bird. "I think we need to go to plan B."

"What's plan B?" Marigold kicked a rock out of the way and peered down the path, wishing a train would come.

"Call for the ghost children," Lightning said.

Marigold frowned and started once again down the path,

anxious to get to Granny's. "You know how they are," she said over her shoulder. "Those ghost children won't do anything unless I give them something in return. Guaranteed they're going to want to come with us to Granny's, and that's definitely the last thing I need right now."

Lightning hurried after her and panted, "Y-You mean we have to *walk*? The e-entire *way*? To *Granny's*?"

She stopped and waited. The dragon caught up and mopped his brow. Marigold knew he wasn't used to moving so fast and she'd have to slow down. At this rate, it would be midnight by the time they made it to the old cabbage's cottage. "I guess you're right," she said, then tossed a handful of gumdrops in the air. Out of nowhere, the ghost children appeared, circling above her head like seagulls at the beach, expertly catching the candy and gobbling it up. They playfully grabbed at her pockets for more. Marigold had never been so happy to see them.

A ghost girl swished past. "Your star is blinking, Marigold."

"I know, and it won't stop. I'm on my way to Granny Cabbage's to get some advice," Marigold answered. "By any chance, could you call a train to get me there faster?"

"I can get the train to take us *all* to Granny's!" the ghost girl said excitedly.

"We love visiting Granny—she has the best candy," her ghost brother chimed in. "Can we go with you?"

"Not today." Marigold gave Lightning her "I told you so" look. She could just see herself with a gaggle of ghost children nagging her for a story and candy while she was trying to get advice from Granny.

"But, Marigold, it will take you hours to get there unless you go by train," one of them said coyly.

"Okay, here's the deal." Marigold was used to negotiating with the ghost children. "I'll give you candy and tell you the best story ever if you call the train to take Lightning and me to Granny's."

The only thing the ghost children loved more than candy was one of Marigold's stories. They squealed with delight and quickly gathered around. Marigold doled out jelly beans. "Do I have your word you'll call the train?" she said before she began.

"You have our word!" the oldest ghost girl promised.

"Tell us the story!" the others shouted, eager for her to start.

Satisfied they would keep their word (to a certain extent—ghosts could be very tricky), Marigold began, "Once upon a time . . ." But right away she was interrupted by a strange rustling sound in the bushes. "Did you hear that, Lightning?" Marigold whispered. They were in Spookety Forest, where anything could happen.

Even the ghost children watched tensely and barely moved.

Marigold and Lightning remained very still. "Shhh." She held a finger to her lips. "Look." A small shadow flickered about in the murky wood, darting from tree to tree.

"It's a shadow boy," Marigold whispered in awe.

"It's a shadow boy!" the ghosts shrieked. There was nothing they were more afraid of than shadow children. They instantly disappeared.

Marigold, on the other hand, knew the creatures were completely harmless, though she'd never seen one before.

"Hello, shadow boy," she said in a soft voice.

The shadow boy came into view and the next moment vanished. Marigold forgot her haste to get to Granny's and held out her hand, hoping he would come to her. "I'm Marigold Star. Let's be friends."

"What's a friend?" the shadow boy said.

Marigold strained her eyes to see, but the shadow boy was shrouded by the forest's cloak of darkness. She felt a pang of sadness for him that he didn't even know what a friend was. "A friend is someone you like no matter what," she replied.

The shadow boy's voice sounded like it was coming from somewhere high in the treetops now. "You mean even if they are super scary looking?"

"Yes, even if they are super scary looking." Marigold looked upward to see if she could find him. "A friend is someone you always have fun with."

Thump!

Marigold was startled to see a box lying in the grass at her feet. She leaned over to have a look. The title of the game was in big red-and-white, candy-striped lettering. "Candy Land?"

"We can have fun," the shadow boy said.

Marigold studied the picture of a gingerbread house with lollipops growing out of the grass and gumdrops hanging off a tree—nothing so unusual. In Bramblycrumbly there were trees and meadows where just these sorts of candy grew wild. No, that wasn't what bothered Marigold. It was the *children* depicted on the box, because she was certain they were *humans*.

Marigold had heard at great length from every teacher she'd ever had as well as her parents that humans were awful creatures from a place far, far away that no one from Bramblycrumbly should ever have anything to do with.

"Will you play Candy Land with me?" the shadow boy said hesitantly.

"Wherever did you get this game?" Marigold asked.

"I—I found it." The shadow boy sounded as if he might cry. "It was stuck in the brambles."

Marigold glanced nervously at Lightning. "I wouldn't touch that thing with a ten-foot pole," the dragon muttered.

Marigold backed away from the box as if it were contagious.

"Never mind," the shadow boy said sadly. "You don't have to play."

Marigold called to where he had slunk under a bush. She'd hurt his feelings—the last thing she'd meant to do!

A moment later, the ghosts reappeared. "Thank goodness *he's* gone." They shuddered collectively.

Marigold tried to explain. "He only wants to be friends—"

"*Friends?*" the ghosts all shouted at once. "Never!" They swirled around in a mass of white, all talking at once. "Quick! Tell us the story before that fiend comes back!"

Marigold cringed. She knew the shadow boy was close enough to hear everything. If only she could get them to see how nice and friendly he really was! This gave her an idea. She handed out peanut brittle, and the ghost children settled down and listened with rapt attention.

"Once upon a time . . . ," Marigold said, "there was a shadow boy who wandered about in Spookety Forest—"

"No-o-o-o-o!" the ghosts yelled, terrified. They huddled closer together and listened with wide, serious eyes.

Marigold continued. "This shadow boy lived in Spookety Cave and was said to be the scariest shadow anyone ever saw. He was in the shape of a creature with pointy fangs, sharp claws, and a long slithery tail. In fact, he was so terrifying that everyone called him Super Scary Shadow Boy."

The ghosts listened, barely moving, their peanut brittle untouched.

"What everyone didn't know was that Super Scary Shadow Boy was loaded with magic powers!" Marigold said. "And this shadow boy loved ghosts too. He would always stay near them, ready at a moment's notice to rescue one if they ever needed him. So, one day a ghost child wandered too close to the Human World."

"Wow! Really?" a ghost girl called out. "The Human World is scary!"

"Scarier than you think," Marigold said. She called to mind the surprising fact she'd read in school and added it. "When the little ghost got to the Human World, no one could see him because he was invisible."

"Wait. What?" The ghost children were puzzled. Their mouths hung open, and they looked like someone had thrown a bucket of cold water on them. "Ghosts are invisible in the Human World? Why?"

"Because *humans* are afraid of ghosts," Marigold replied astutely.

"Afraid? Of us? We don't have long pointy tails or fangs or claws. We're not scary, are we, Marigold Star? Are we?" They were becoming more and more worked up.

Lightning nudged her to finish the story, and she was anxious to get to Granny's too!

"SH-U-U-U-SH!" Marigold scolded. They finally

quieted, and she spoke quickly. "So, like I said, the little ghost was invisible in the Human World—he couldn't even see himself—but Super Scary Shadow Boy had followed right behind. One of his magic powers was that he had super-duper vision. He could see the ghost, so he led him back to Bramblycrumbly, safe and sound. The little ghost told all the other ghosts, and from that day on they were no longer scared of the shadow boy. They all became good friends and lived happily ever after." Marigold stole a look to see that the shadow boy was still in his hiding place. He must have heard everything.

The ghost children sat with glum looks on their faces.

It was not exactly the reaction she had hoped for. Seeing them unmoved by her story, she added, "Super Scary Shadow Boy was the most incredible superhero in all of Bramblycrumbly. . . . The end!" Marigold caught Lightning's eye, and he tapped his wristwatch in a gesture that meant they needed to get going.

"Now will you *please* get the train—a deal's a deal!" the dragon said.

"B-o-o-o-o-o!" one ghost called. "B-o-o-o-o!" the rest joined in.

Marigold held up her hands to quiet them. "Don't you see?" she tried to explain. "Just because someone is scary looking doesn't mean you wouldn't like him or that he's not super nice."

"That's a stupid story," a ghost boy said. "Marigold Star is making it all up." As they floated away, Marigold could still hear them grumbling about her tale. She was greatly relieved to see a beam of light coming right toward her. At least they had made good on their word.

"*Woo! Woo!*" the train whistle sounded. The train was drenched in white fog, and tendrils of mist flew from its wheels. The brakes screeched as it glided to a stop. The door slid open.

"All aboard!" the conductor called. "Next stop, Granny Cabbage's!"

The brakes were released with a loud *whooosh*.

Marigold and Lightning made their way through the cars of the train. Red-velvet with gold-fringed curtains hung at the windows and a slight mist clung to the floor.

Marigold slid into a seat, and Lightning sat across from her.

"Is it still blinking?" she asked. She was too nervous to look.

"It is," the dragon replied.

They sat in silence until Marigold said, "Do you think I could be coming down with something?" Without waiting for the dragon's response, she said, "Or maybe I'm allergic to the strawberry jam I had on my muffin this morning instead of honey like I always have."

"I doubt it's that," Lightning said.

Normally this was her favorite part of the trip, when she could sit back, close her eyes, and feel the train grow weightless while it ascended over the tops of trees, into the sky, where it would soar between banks of clouds. But not today. She worried and wondered if the old cabbage lady could even help her.

Marigold leaned her head against the window and sighed. "I have a lot of problems."

3

A WARNING FROM GRANNY CABBAGE

The train pulled away, leaving Marigold and Lightning in a lovely glade powdered with wild daisies. They were just outside Spookety Forest, right by Granny's cottage. Red, pink, and white roses covered the limestone walls. Lavender and mint grew plentiful in flower boxes beneath windows with diamond-shaped panes of glass that glinted in the sun. All was hushed except for the enchanted song of wind chimes that hung from the branch of a silver pear tree. Tiny yellow parakeets watched like sentinels from their perches and a moment later flew as a group to the house, as if to notify Granny that she had company.

Marigold's eyes rose to the chimney, where a puff of smoke meandered skyward. That meant the old cabbage lady was home.

"I sure hope she's not busy." Marigold knocked on the door.

"I sure hope not," Lightning said.

Everyone knew that Granny Cabbage had hundreds of friends and that they came from far and wide for help. Granny had an answer for everything, from tonics for whatever ailed you to the proper storage of magic beans and the care and feeding of a golden goose. She could thatch a roof, cure a bunion, and make porridge that actually tasted good.

Luckily, today she was not busy and appeared at the door right away.

If you could imagine an extraordinarily large cabbage with two eyes, a cabbage leaf for a nose, the squiggly edge between leaves for a mouth, stubby legs and arms, and all of this wrapped in a long shawl, that would be Granny. Granny's face broke into a wide crinkly grin as soon as she saw Marigold.

"I'm sorry." Marigold held out her empty hands. She visited Granny Cabbage once a week to bring her a blueberry crumble from the Bramblycrumbly Bakery, which was known for the best crumble in the land.

"Never mind that." Granny eyed Marigold's blinking star, and a mysterious smile stole across her lips. "It looks like you could use some advice."

"I could. I have five problems, Granny," Marigold replied.

"Five!" Lightning stressed.

The old cabbage hurried Marigold and her dragon inside. Birdhouses hung from low rafters along with bunches of dried jasmine, horseradish, garlic, and other herbs. On the swept dirt floor were gardening tools and several quarts of apple cider vinegar that Granny used for just about everything. Lightning pulled his tail around him, careful not to knock any of the knickknacks and trinkets off the shelves that lined the walls.

Marigold got on the stuffed chair by the fire that burned merrily in the corner. She tucked her feet under her while Lightning found a nice soft spot on a cushion beside her. Granny lowered herself into the other chair, placed her feet on a plump burlap sack of wood chips, and laced her gnarled fingers across her chest. "Tell me all your problems, child," she said in a shaky voice, for she was very old.

The words tumbled out of Marigold's mouth.

Granny listened intently, saying things from time to time like, "Hmmm," and "Oh, my," and "Very interesting."

"And it's just not the same at home anymore," Marigold finished.

"Oh?" Granny had a questioning look on her face.

"Petal," Lightning said in a grave tone.

Marigold frowned. "If I went off into the forest and lived in a shack with Lightning, my parents would never even notice."

"Betel nuts!" Granny exclaimed.

Marigold and Lightning sat up, slightly startled.

"You were born with a star over your head, Marigold, and the star is never wrong," Granny said firmly. "It's a sure sign that you are marked for greatness."

"I know all that, Granny." Marigold stood and paced in front of the fire. "It's just that I can't do any of the spells, and I can't even get my magic wand to work right. I don't understand what's wrong with me." She reached for the wand to show Granny, but her pocket was empty, and then she remembered that the last time she had the wand was to show Bob the Invisibility Spell. Probably Lightning had taken it from her for safekeeping. When she asked her dragon, sure enough, he produced it once again.

Marigold laughed, feeling a little foolish, but Granny had a stern look on her face. "Hasn't anyone ever told you, child, that you're supposed to always carry your *own* magic wand?"

"Yes, but—"

"No buts." Granny shook her finger at Marigold. "You're old enough to always know where it is."

"But look, Granny, it won't even sparkle the way it's supposed to." Marigold held the wand in one hand. It hardly radiated even a dull light. She shook it a few times with little change. Marigold flopped back in the chair and folded her arms. "Anyway, why should I care where it is?"

"Because you might lose it!" All the birds came out of their houses and began to tweet loudly. The old woman hushed them with a wave of her hand. She turned back to Marigold. "Never lose your magic wand," she warned.

Marigold had heard it a million times from her mother, who was afraid that a hobgoblin might get it—everyone in Bramblycrumbly had one or two living in their house. Hobgoblins, known as "brownies," were small wrinkled creatures who wore brown cloaks and who came out only at night to steal honey and porridge. They always gave something in return, in the form of a task like washing the dishes or polishing the silver, and they were harmless . . . until they got ahold of someone's magic wand. Brownies never thought twice about wishing for a river of honey or porridge to flow right through the middle of someone's house! Once a hobgoblin came into possession of a magic wand, it could take a dozen wizards to get it back.

Marigold tried to redeem herself. "I know, Granny, it's because of the brownies, and—"

Granny interrupted, "*Not* just the brownies, girl. The wand could end up in the hands of humans."

"*Humans?*" Marigold had never thought of that. Humans were in an entirely different world. A world that was difficult to get to and that she never planned on visiting if she could help it. Why should she worry about humans getting ahold of her wand?

Suddenly the room became cold, and the fire sputtered as if it might go out. Granny whispered in a raspy voice, "Come closer, child." Marigold knelt beside the old cabbage while Lightning crept forward to listen as well.

"If your wand ever got into the hands of a human, something terrible could happen."

"What?" Marigold whispered.

Granny refused to say. "Never mind what!" The old cabbage rose stiffly and hobbled over to her shelf. She absently held her chin in one hand while the other hand lightly brushed over the objects: a baseball, a rag doll, a stuffed bear, a snow globe. There were too many to count.

Marigold craned her neck to see. "What are all those things?"

"It's my collection—gifts from friends of mine when I was exactly your age." Granny had a faraway look in her eyes as she spoke. She paused at an empty spot on the shelf. "But there's one missing." She sighed and shuffled back to her seat. "My collection will never be complete now."

"Why not?" Marigold asked.

Granny waved the question away. "Just remember, Marigold, don't *ever* lose your magic wand."

"I—I promise." Marigold gripped the wand now with all her might. "I won't rely on Lightning to keep track of it. . . . I'll be more careful." She raised her eyes to see the light from the star still blinking. "I'll even try harder to learn to fly and get my spells right." Marigold bit her lip. "It's just that— Oh, Granny." She sighed. "Even if I do learn to fly and stop making so many mistakes with my spells, everyone still expects me to become something so great. . . ." Marigold's voice faded.

The room was quiet except for the sound of the crackling fire. The old cabbage lady smiled softly. "You're a great friend, Marigold."

"What's so great about being a great friend?" Marigold asked.

"Everything." Granny smiled. She studied Marigold for such a long time that Marigold and Lightning exchanged worried glances. Then Granny nodded as if she had just made up her mind about something. "You do not have five problems!" she announced. "You only have *one*!"

"W-what is it?" Marigold stammered. She was almost afraid to ask.

"You have a magic power . . . and you need to discover what it is." Then Granny reached under her shawl and took out a small book. It was worn and curled at the edges, but there was no mistaking the title written in gold leaf on the cover: *Bramblycrumbly Book of Spells.* "This was mine when I was your age." She tapped the top of the book with a finger. "Everything you need to help you discover your magic power is right in here."

40

"But Granny—" Marigold wasn't convinced. "You've just given me another problem. Now I have six—"

"No," Granny insisted. "You have only one problem!" She rose from her chair, signaling the end of the conversation.

Marigold didn't dare say another word.

"Shouldn't you be home by now, dearie?" the old cabbage said in a sweeter tone, and then she pressed the book of spells into Marigold's hand.

4

10 WIGGLYRAMBLY WAY

Marigold walked slowly down the lane toward home with Lightning at her side. She passed little bungalows, in front of which thick ivy and brambly vines covered picket fences and trellised gates. One home was in the shape of an acorn; another looked like a giant pumpkin; yet another, a gourd; there was even a house in the shape of an enormous mushroom sprouting out of the ground. Marigold and Lightning lived in the last house, 10 Wigglyrambly Way, which looked like a teapot. When they got close, there was no mistaking the loathsome sound of a wailing baby.

Petal. Who else?

"Hi, Mom. Hi, Dad," Marigold called as soon as she passed through the Dutch door into the kitchen. The kitchen was a round room with stone walls and two round windows. Pots and pans hung from iron hooks that stuck out of wooden beams in the ceiling.

Petal howled her head off, locked into her high chair, which hovered three feet off the floor. Her father, Horace, looked on, scowling. Dressed in a long gray robe with an ample hood, he was a weather wizard with periwinkle-blue eyes that could stop a howling blizzard with an icy stare or create a small tornado in a mason jar with a blink. The only thing he seemed powerless over was his baby daughter, Petal.

"WAAAAAAAAH!" Her face was an angry red, her mouth a black, gaping hole. Her feet kicked, and her tiny hands, balled up into mighty fists, pounded the air.

Marigold's mother, Tulip, stood with her arms folded. She had short-cropped hair like the pixies—that was a popular style in Bramblycrumbly. The front of her gossamer gown was spotted with mashed yam, and her crystal tiara teetered to one side. She pushed it into place with the back of her hand. "I told you, Horace, she doesn't like the Levitating High Chair Spell."

"She liked it yesterday," Horace said defensively. He flicked a large clump of yam off his sleeve.

Tulip shook her head. "No, dear—that was the Soaring Spoon Spell, remember?"

"Hi, Mom. Hi, Dad," Marigold repeated.

"They're not going to hear you, you know," Lightning said. He opened the cupboard and took out a bowl. "I'm starving," he muttered.

Marigold could see it was going to be another night of cereal for dinner, and she got busy making a bowl for herself as well.

"WAH! WAH! WAAAAAAAAH!" Petal screamed.

"Look, honey bunny," Tulip called. She snapped her fingers, and a silver spoon sparkled into view. "It's your favorite—the Soaring Spoon!" The spoon spun into life. It scooped up some yams and roared around the room, swooping and looping the loop. The yam bowl raced behind it to keep up. After three turns around the kitchen, the spoon came to a screeching halt right by Petal. She shook her head and clamped her mouth shut.

"Open wide," Tulip sang.

Petal swatted the spoon, and it clattered to the ground. She pushed the bowl away with all her strength, and it turned upside down. Mashed yam hit the floor with a resounding *splat*!

"WAAAAAAAAH!" Petal cried even louder.

Marigold's mother threw up her hands and collapsed in a chair.

"So much for the Soaring Spoon Spell," Marigold's father said, and stuck his fingers in his ears.

Marigold turned to Lightning. "Can you believe this?"

The dragon finished his cereal and put the bowl in the sink. "It's definitely not like it used to be around here."

Marigold finished hers as well and wiped her mouth. "I don't care what Granny says. I still think we should get our own place in the forest."

Lightning suggested, "Why not try getting their attention again—louder this time?"

Marigold took a deep breath and, as loud as she could, yelled, "HI, MOM! HI, DAD!"

Suddenly Petal stopped crying. "Do you hear that?" Marigold's parents said with disbelief. "Ahhhhh, peace and quiet," they whispered.

Petal stared at Marigold's star and pointed. "Mawigohd blinky!"

Both parents turned to their other daughter in surprise. "Marigold!" they said. "There you are!"

Marigold's star blinked. Off. On. Off. On. Off. On.

Petal giggled with glee.

"It's not funny," Marigold said angrily. "It won't stop!"

"She's right. Her star's been doing that all day," Lightning added with concern.

"I'm sure it's nothing," her mother said breezily.

Marigold frowned. "Maybe it'll go out—I hope it does!"

Her father looked surprised. "But, honey, it's a sure sign—"

"—of greatness," her mother finished in a hushed tone.

"But I'm not great at anything!" Marigold cried.

"Maybe you just need to apply yourself a little more," her father said gently.

"Or practice with your magic wand a few more times a day," her mother suggested.

Her father raised a bushy eyebrow and asked, "How's that Thunder Spell coming along, hmmm?"

"Not so good," Marigold replied. She was terrible at weather spells. Marigold knew she would never grow up to be a weather wizard like her father.

Marigold's mother held an apple in each hand. "Which one is poison, dear?"

Marigold hesitated. "Um . . . that one . . . no . . . that one . . . no . . . that one?"

Her mother shook her head. Marigold knew she would never grow up to be a fairy god-doctor like her mother either.

Marigold's father said, "Well, at least you've learned how to do the Invisibility Spell by now?"

"N-Not exactly," Marigold stammered.

Her parents looked at each other in dismay.

Marigold shrugged. "So that just proves it—I'm not so great, after all."

"Pumpkin seeds!" Her mother tossed the apples in the air, and they vanished. "You are going to be great at something that we can't even imagine yet!"

"Something rare and incredibly wondrous," her father added confidently.

"All you need is a little more practice, honey," her mother said.

"Start by learning the Invisibility Spell, dear," her father said. "I know you can do it."

"The star is never wrong!" both her parents exclaimed.

Marigold shuffled out of the kitchen, her eyes on the floor. On the way to her room, she could still see the walls light up every time her star blinked. It was so annoying. "Something rare and incredibly wondrous," she muttered to herself. "That'll be the day."

Lightning pushed open the heavy wooden door to her bedroom. Marigold climbed on her bed, which was tucked into a corner beside the window. The star continued to blink like a warning beacon. She sat cross-legged on top of the patchwork quilt. "I'm a hopeless case, Lightning."

"You're too hard on yourself, Marigold." Lightning patted her arm, and she could tell he felt sorry for her. It made her feel like crying.

"Can *you* do the Invisibility Spell?" She sniffed.

The dragon lowered his eyes.

Marigold had a feeling she wasn't going to like what her dragon was about to tell her.

"Okay! So I can do the Invisibility Spell," he finally admitted. "So what?"

"So what?" Marigold held both hands out. "I'm the only person in all of Bramblycrumbly who can't do the Invisibility Spell. . . . I'll bet even Petal will learn it before me!"

What an awful thought. Marigold suddenly felt lightheaded. The cereal she'd just eaten churned in her stomach. She pulled the *Bramblycrumbly Book of Spells* out of her pocket.

She knew there was no other way around this. She didn't

care what she had to do to learn this spell—no way was Petal going to learn it before she did. She made up her mind. She took a deep breath. "That's it!"

"That's what?" Lightning asked.

"I'm learning that spell!" Marigold announced.

"Okay," Lightning said.

"If it's the last thing I do!" Marigold added.

"Okay," Lightning said.

"In fact—I'm never leaving this room! Okay?"

"Okay."

"Ever—till I learn it!"

"Okay."

Marigold stuck out her chin. "Okay!"

5

THE INVIS-O-FRIEND SPELL

Lightning had his own bed on the other side of the room, next to a small fireplace that he conveniently kept lit with his breath whenever it was cold. He curled up on the bed and sighed.

Marigold got busy and thumbed through Granny's book. There was all kinds of information, ranging from recipes and advice to lists of magic words for protection against things like your pot of gold being nabbed by a gnome to little-known facts such as the life span of goblins. The book was so fascinating that Marigold could have stayed up all night reading it, but she had an assignment to do, so she focused on the section marked, "Spells."

There were spells to make someone sleep for a hundred years and spells to wake them up. There were spells to pass through fire unharmed or turn a ragged dress into a ball gown. One particular spell caught Marigold's eye, and she read with great interest.

THE FLYING SPELL

The Flying Spell is the oldest one in the book and extremely easy to master, even for the youngest. Though a word of caution: the Flying Spell does require a suspension of disbelief—especially during the leaping portion—more suited to the very young. The older one becomes, the more difficult the Flying Spell becomes. . . .

"Great," Marigold said flatly.

Suddenly there was a knock at the window. It was her friend Mrs. Moon. "Hi, Marigold. What are you doing?"

"I'm trying to learn how to become invisible. I'm not leaving my room until I do," Marigold said firmly.

"That's the spirit!" the owl replied. "Did you solve any of your problems?"

"Granny Cabbage says my only problem is that I have a magic power and I have to find out what it is," Marigold said. "What do you think my magic power could be?"

The owl knew right away. "You always say just the right thing to make me feel better—maybe your magic power is that you can read minds!"

"That's an interesting idea," Marigold said, but she knew that wasn't her magic power. "Thanks, Mrs. Moon!"

"Good luck!" said the owl, and she flew away.

Marigold picked up the spell book again, but a moment later there came the tapping sound of pebbles being thrown at her window. It was another friend, Bob the Woodcutter's Son.

"Did you solve any of your problems?" he called up to her.

Marigold told him what Granny Cabbage had said. "What do you think my magic power is, Bob?"

"I think you have the power to make any chore seem like fun," Bob said.

"That's so nice of you to say, Bob." Marigold was pleased to hear it, but she didn't even think that was a real magic power.

"Come down and help me gather some wood," he added.

Marigold shook her head. "I'm not leaving this room until I learn to become invisible!"

Bob wished her good luck and left to finish his chore.

Marigold went back to her book, but right away her two good friends Daisy and Rosie showed up. When Marigold asked what they thought her magic power could be, they said, "You're good at sharing—you always let us go for rides on Lightning. Come down and let's go for a ride!"

Soon after, Lily and Iris stopped by because they had heard that their friend Marigold had some problems, and they wanted to help. So did the vegetable people Chickpea, Ginger, and Parsnip. Everyone had ideas of what Marigold's magic power was, and everyone thought she should come out and play to take her mind off her problems.

Marigold politely declined the offers. She was anxious to learn the Invisibility Spell and said good night to all her friends. Even Lightning was asleep by now.

"At least it's finally quiet." She sighed and got to work. Of course, she'd been taught the Invisibility Spell—every child in Bramblycrumbly knew it by the time they were six—but so far, she'd never been able to get it right. She searched Granny's book to make sure she was doing it correctly. Before too long she found what she was looking for.

THE INVISIBILITY SPELL

This is the EASIEST spell in this book!

STEP ONE: *Hold magic wand firmly in right hand.*

STEP TWO: *Take right foot off ground.*

STEP THREE: *Rub stomach with left hand in a circular motion and tap head with magic wand.*

STEP FOUR: *Cross eyes.*

STEP FIVE: *State CLEARLY what you want to be invisible.*

Marigold took out her magic wand.
She placed it carefully on the bed and stared at it.
She did not like the magic wand.
Bad things happened when she tried to use it.

Just last week, she had said to it, "Magic Wand . . . make us a snack!" Instantly she and Lightning had ended up in the nastiest giant's cave in Bramblycrumbly and had to be rescued by the fire department.

Marigold picked the wand up off the bed. She held the wand firmly in her right hand, which trembled slightly. She raised her right foot off the ground and wobbled as she rubbed her stomach in a circular motion with her left hand. She tapped her head, but when she got to the part where she was supposed to cross her eyes, she lost her balance. Just before she tumbled to the floor, she blurted out, "Magic Wand . . . be invisible!"

POOF!

Marigold gasped. For the first time *ever*, the Invisibility Spell had actually worked!

There was only one thing. . . .

It had worked on her magic wand, which was now invisible.

Marigold stared in disbelief at her right hand, where the wand had been a second ago. "Where did it go?"

She searched frantically through the bedclothes. No wand.

She looked under the bed. No wand.

She got on her hands and knees and felt every square inch of the floor. No wand.

She sat on the edge of her bed, breathing hard from the effort. "Do you think the brownies got it, Lightning?" she asked the dragon, who was awake now from all the commotion.

He had a very good nose, which always came in handy for times like this. He sniffed loudly. Marigold waited, her heart pounding, until he finally concluded that he did not smell brownies.

Marigold fell backward and lay flat on her back with her hands over her face. She'd be lucky if *just* the brownies had gotten it. "You realize, Lightning, that Granny warned me just a little while ago not to lose my wand."

"Uh-huh," Lightning said.

"And that I promised I wouldn't," she continued.

"Uh-huh," Lightning said again.

"And that because I've lost it, something terrible could happen."

"Yes, but on the bright side, that's only if it gets into the hands of a brownie, which it didn't—or a human," Lightning reminded her.

"And that could never happen, right, Lightning?" Marigold's eyes filled with tears. "I mean, there's no way—right, Lightning?" Marigold was getting more and more upset. "I promised Granny I wouldn't lose it, and now I have! I promised! I promised!"

"Calm down, Marigold." Lightning was used to getting into fixes with her, and this was just another. "Maybe it's easier to find an invisible wand if you yourself are invisible."

"Do you think?" Marigold brightened.

"Let's see what Granny's book says," Lightning suggested.

They both looked at where it had fallen onto the floor next to the bed.

Marigold picked up the book and it was opened to a page. "Wow," she said softly.

"It's almost like it knew," Lightning whispered.

The page said:

> It's easier to find a magic wand if you yourself are invisible!*
>
> *see next page, Invisibility Spells

"Except you'll probably need a wand to do the spell," Lightning muttered.

Marigold turned the page to see:

!!!NO WAND REQUIRED!!!

"WOW! Look, Lightning!"

The page said:

**** INVIS-O-FRIEND SPELL ****

This spell will make you invisible to all but that one very special friend who needs you the most.*

STEP ONE: *Stand in center of room away from any movable objects.*

STEP TWO: *Repeat the following words as many times as needed:*

"Izzable dizzable, make me invisible to all but one.

Send me to the most friendless of friends—unless I've never been a friend before."

STEP THREE: *Close eyes.*

*you must have prior experience as a friend to complete this spell!

"This is perfect!" Marigold could have jumped for joy. "I'll be invisible *and* find my magic wand!"

Lightning didn't look so sure. "But, Marigold, it doesn't say specifically about finding a lost wand. And I don't like that part about you being sent 'to the most friendless of friends.'"

Marigold rolled her eyes. "It means that I'll be invisible to everyone but you, silly—the one who needs me the most!"

"But—" Lightning said.

"Stop being so negative," Marigold said. "Watch." She stood in the center of the room, repeated the words, and closed her eyes.

"See? It's fine!" she said. "You can still see me, right, Lightning? Lightning?"

6

WINNIE

"Who's Lightning?" a voice said.

Marigold opened her eyes to see that she was in someone else's room. A black crystal chandelier hung from the ceiling over a canopied bed, where a girl who looked to be about Marigold's age sat scowling at her. She wore green pajamas and had a little pug nose that made her look like she smelled something bad. Marigold's wand glittered in the girl's hand. "I *said*, who's Lightning?" the girl repeated.

"H-He's my dragon," Marigold stammered. Except for the unpleasant expression on her face, this girl resembled the children in the picture on the Candy Land box. "I'm Marigold Star. Are you a . . . *human*?"

"Of course I am—don't be ridiculous." The girl stuck her tongue out.

Marigold tried to speak, but nothing came out. How had she ended up in a human girl's bedroom? "But—but humans aren't supposed to be in Bramblycrumbly!"

"Bramby-whaty?" the girl asked.

"Bramblycrumbly—you're not supposed to be here, human!"

"I am too supposed to be here." The girl huffed. "*You're* the one who's not supposed to be here!"

Marigold suddenly had the worst feeling. "Where. Is. Here?"

The girl rolled her eyes. "The world," she said impatiently.

"The *Human World*?" Marigold's voice rose in panic.

"Like hello? What other world is there?" the girl barked.

Marigold thought she might pass out until she realized she had momentarily stopped breathing. The girl stared at her idly, rolling the handle of the wand between her thumb and fingers. The star twinkled ominously.

"You've got my magic wand. Could you give it back?" Even to Marigold her voice came out sounding scared and unsure.

"No way—I've been wanting one of these things for, like, forever." The girl waved the magic wand, and Marigold couldn't help noticing that it lit up the room in a way it never did when she used it. It was bad enough that she had lost her magic wand, but it had ended up in the worst of all places. It was the same place where Granny Cabbage had just told her something terrible could happen. And that place was—in the hands of a *human*!

The girl scrunched up her nose. "You've got a star over your head."

Marigold replied, "I know, it's blinking, and—"

"No, it's not," said the girl.

"Yes, it is," Marigold insisted, but when she looked up, she was shocked to see that it had stopped blinking! It was shining steadily and brightly just like it always had— and that was at least one good thing. "Everyone thinks my star is supposed to be a sure sign of greatness, except that—"

"Well, I don't like it," the girl snapped. "I don't like your hat either—take it off."

"I can't take it off," Marigold said indignantly.

Without warning the girl reached forward and grabbed what she thought was Marigold's hat.

"OW!" Marigold yelled. "It's not a hat—it's my hair!" She

rubbed her head. "That wasn't very nice, *human!*"

"My name isn't *human*. It's Winnie. And of course it wasn't nice—I'm the most unfriendly girl in town," she said proudly.

"You mean you don't have any friends, Winnie?" Marigold was astonished. It seemed to her that even humans needed friends.

"Nope," she replied.

"But you've got to have at least one friend," Marigold insisted.

"Yeah? Why?" Winnie asked.

"Because . . . because . . . it's so much fun to have friends!" Marigold said.

"Not for me." Winnie folded her arms and shook her head. "I don't like anyone, especially you!" She stuck out her tongue again.

"But everyone likes me!" Marigold exclaimed. "Even the goblins and the trolls."

The girl narrowed her eyes dangerously at Marigold. "Did you just call me a goblin?"

Luckily, Marigold didn't have to answer, because just then there was a knock at the door. A woman popped her head into the room. She had a pug nose, jet-black bangs, and a long tight braid identical to Winnie's. She could be no one else but the girl's mother. "Who are you talking to, sweetums?" she asked.

Winnie pointed to Marigold. "Her."

"Who?" Her mother looked all around.

"Her!"

"But there's no one there, Winnie Binnie," her mother replied.

Marigold's mouth dropped open. Could it be possible? "Ask her what she means," Marigold said excitedly.

"What do you mean?" Winnie asked.

"I mean, you are talking to someone and there are only you and I in this room," her mother replied.

Marigold could hardly contain herself. She skipped around the room shouting, "You can't see me because I'm INVISIBLE!" She waved a hand in the lady's face, and when she had no reaction, Marigold did a cartwheel in the middle of the room.

"Okay, so you didn't just see somebody do a cartwheel in the middle of the room?" Winnie said.

"No, silly dilly. You have a big day tomorrow. Now go to

sleep!" Winnie's mother turned off the light and shut the door.

Marigold was so happy she could have flown if she'd known how. "I'm invisible! I'm invisible!"

"Not to me." Winnie traced a circle in the air with the tip of the wand, leaving a trail of sparkles.

Marigold could feel her confidence rising. Maybe she wasn't so hopeless after all! Maybe it wouldn't be that difficult to get her magic wand back. Lightning would be so proud of her—she couldn't wait to show him that she was invisible.

Winnie was speaking. "And just so you know, I never cry, and . . . I'm not afraid of ghosts."

"I'm not a ghost—and please be careful with that wand." Marigold could feel her sudden sense of well-being begin to fade. "It never works the way it's supposed to."

"Oh yeah? Well, we'll see about that." Winnie waved the wand over her head. "Magic wand . . . give me a green cape with a big gold star on the back!"

BOINGO! POOF!

Marigold's star lit the room just enough for her to see the girl suddenly wearing a long fluffy green cape with a glittery star on the back. "How'd you do that?" Marigold exclaimed.

"Easy! Watch this," Winnie said. "Magic wand . . . give me a bag of delicious candy!"

BING! BANG! BOOM!

Marigold was shocked to see a bag of candy appear in Winnie's hand.

This had definitely gone too far. She had to put a stop to it at once. She held out her hand and wiggled her fingers. "Give me the wand, Winnie. Please?"

Winnie gave her an evil grin and pointed the wand at her own feet. "Magic wand . . . give me white sneakers with green polka dots!"

BONGO! SHRUSH!

Just like that, she was wearing green polka-dot sneakers. She jumped up and clicked her heels. Marigold looked on helplessly—she just *had* to get her wand back, but how? She didn't have Lightning to help her or Granny Cabbage to give her advice, but she still had Granny's spell book! She reached for the book, and it opened to exactly where she'd left off. By the light of her star she read:

THE INVIS-O-FRIEND SPELL

Great. It was the spell that had landed her in this room in the first place. But then she noticed something. Below the spell was one little word: "over."

"Over?" Marigold muttered to herself, and she turned the page to see that it meant there was a lot more to this Invis-O-Friend Spell than she had thought.

The book said:

> In order to complete the Invis-O-Friend Spell, Invis-O-Friend may not use a magic wand to simply wish for completion. Instead, Invis-O-Friend must share laughter, joy, advice, and sorrow with visible friend.
>
> Failure to complete the above spell by no later than the ninth birthday* of said visible friend will result in detainment of Invis-O-Friend in Human World forever.

P.S. Invis-O-Friend may not confide in visible friend about the terms of this spell until spell is completed. Violations of these terms will also result in detainment of Invis-O-Friend in Human World forever.

*ninth birthday: see "Lost or Missing Wands"

Detainment in Human World *forever*? Marigold turned to the page on "Lost or Missing Wands" and read on with a sense of growing alarm.

LOST OR MISSING WANDS

If Invis-O-Friend loses a magic wand, it can result in the phenomenon known as "SEEPAGE"*

Marigold turned the page and there it was. . . .

*SEEPAGE: When characters, places, and/ or objects spontaneously appear in a world other than their own.

71

The Good News!

If this *Seepage* occurred as a result of an Invis-O-Friend losing a magic wand, then at the completion of the Invis-O-Friend Spell and upon the retrieval of the magic wand with visible friend where *Seepage* originated, said *Seepage* will auto-reverse, i.e., all characters, places, and/or objects will automatically return to their appropriate worlds.

ALSO: Seepage does not affect the age* of visible friend because technically they are still in the Human World.

*age: See "Rules for Birthdays."

The Bad News!

If Invis-O-Friend *fails* to complete spell by

visible friend's ninth birthday *AND* does *NOT* recover said magic wand, **Bramblycrumbly will crumble and turn to brambles.**

*P.S. A magic wand IS required to return to Bramblycrumbly from the **Human World***

Have a nice day! ☺

*Human World: see "Rules for Birthdays."

RULES FOR BIRTHDAYS

Be advised: It is VERY important that you know there is a—

Marigold quickly turned the page to see what was "VERY important to know," but on the next page there was only a list of medicinal herbs for baldness. It was a very old book with dog-eared corners and a few pages that were held together only by tape. Indeed, when she checked, there were the telltale ragged edges of several pages that had been torn out! "Very important to know, *very* important know . . . ," Marigold muttered as she leafed through the book while looking for the missing pages in the hope that they'd been shoved between some other pages, but she found nothing. What was so important in these lost pages? Marigold had no idea, but now she knew what Granny meant when she said something terrible could happen if a magic wand got into the hands of a human. If she didn't get her magic wand back, everything in Bramblycrumbly would crumble and turn to brambles. No wonder the old cabbage didn't want to tell her—it was too awful!

Could it be that the only way to keep this from happening was to make friends with this awful human? But what if Marigold didn't have much time to make friends? What if Winnie's birthday was tomorrow?

"When is your ninth birthday, Winnie?" Marigold asked breathlessly.

"Tomorrow," Winnie snapped. "In fact, I'm having a birthday party and you're not invited—no one is!"

Winnie twirled the wand in a sweeping motion. "Magic wand . . . give me a magic flying carpet!"

SWOOSH! BAM!

A magic flying carpet instantly appeared.

"Cut it out, Winnie!" Marigold shouted.

"HA!" Winnie laughed, and pointed the wand at one of the tall windows. "Magic wand . . . open the window next to my bed."

Marigold groaned. At least "Seepage" hadn't occurred. She looked up to see Winnie contemplating her. The girl tapped the air with the magic wand several times and chanted, "Magic wand . . . send me some ghosts!"

7

IZZABLE DIZZABLE

Suddenly the curtains billowed out. The black crystal chandelier swayed and tinkled. A chill, clammy breeze swept through the room, heralding some unseen presence.

Winnie stood with her feet planted, the green cape fluttering out behind her, the wand glittering formidably. "I'm not afraid of you, ghosts!" she exclaimed.

Marigold held her breath.

"Where are we?" a voice said.

"Where are you?" another asked.

"Where am I?" a third cried.

Marigold's heart sank. She had no doubt that these were the very same voices of the ghost children from Bramblycrumbly, who were now in the Human World! "Seepage," she whispered.

True to her promise, Winnie showed off her bravery by making rude noises at the ghosts.

Marigold could feel their gowns brush against her as they gathered around. "Who's that, Marigold Star?" they asked in hushed voices.

"It's Winnie," Marigold replied.

"What's a Winnie?" They wanted to know.

"Winnie is a *human*," she answered.

"A *human*?" they cried.

The pictures on the walls moved seemingly by themselves, and soon all were hanging at odd angles.

"We're in the Human World! That's why we're invisible!" they moaned. "That's why we can't even see ourselves!"

Winnie stamped her foot. "Straighten those pictures on that wall this instant!"

The ghost children gave a hardy tug on her long black braid in answer to her demand. Then one spotted her bag of candy and nipped at it. Before long all the ghosts were circling around her—except Winnie wasn't offering anything. "Get away from my bag of candy!" She swung the wand like a baseball bat.

The ghosts retreated over to Marigold, where they could be heard murmuring in a sulky group.

"The human is so unfriendly—it's because we are invisible, Marigold Star!"

"It's because she can't see how nice we are . . ."

" . . . and that all we want is candy . . ."

" . . . and a story . . ."

"We don't want to be invisible, Marigold Star. *Do* something!"

Marigold could barely speak, let alone answer the ghost children's pleas. They weren't supposed to be here. They had spontaneously appeared in a world other than their own. If only she could get her magic wand away from Winnie, she could wish the ghosts back to Bramblycrumbly!

The room was dark. The ghost children moaned, and the wand sparkled in Winnie's hand. If it hadn't been for her star shining brightly, Marigold thought it would be easy to sneak up behind the girl and grab the wand right out of her hand. Which is exactly what happened. In a flash, the magic wand was snatched—but not by Marigold.

"HEY! Give that back, you!" Winnie yelled.

"Magic wand . . . make these ghosts visible!" a voice said.

KA-BOOM!

The ghosts appeared. Their white, filmy gowns glowed in the dark as they swirled and babbled, happy to be able to see one another again. They bounced on top of the canopied bed as if it were a trampoline. They lifted it off the floor to their gales of laughter and then spun it around a few times.

Winnie hardly noticed. She chased after the magic wand that glittered and bobbed through the dark. She lunged for it, sure that she'd gotten it only to have it appear across the room. Marigold had her eye on it as well, but she found it just as difficult as Winnie to grab. They both thought it was one of the ghosts who had the magic wand. They were both wrong.

"Are you a ghost?" Winnie demanded. "Because if you are—"

"I'm Super Scary Shadow Boy!" a voice proclaimed.

Marigold's star lit the wall where his shadow loomed. The shadow had fangs and claws and a long slithery tail. The ghost children stopped in midair. All laughter ceased. All motion stopped. There was a collective, audible gasp. The ghost children flew around the room, crashing into one another as they all headed to the same place—the window—

which they squeezed through and flew off into the night in terror.

The shadow boy sprang onto the window ledge. "Magic wand, give me wings to fly!" he commanded. Immediately his dark shape sprouted wings, which made him look even scarier. He leaped into the air and was gone.

Winnie raced to the window and leaned out so far it looked as if she might fly out of it too. "Come back here with my wand, Super Scary Shadow Boy!"

Marigold could have said, "*Your* wand? It's *my* wand!" but she was too stunned to speak. In less than half an hour, she'd landed in the Human World, lost her wand to a human and now to a shadow boy, and because of all this, Bramblycrumbly could crumble and turn to brambles in only a matter of hours.

The magic flying carpet floated in the air knee-high before Winnie, ready to do her bidding. "I'm going to get that magic wand back if it's the last thing I do. I'm not afraid of some stupid shadow!" She pointed to the flying carpet. "Get on," she ordered Marigold.

"I don't think this is such a good idea." Marigold eyed the carpet, thinking it looked dangerous.

Winnie shrugged. "Suit yourself." She hopped on the carpet. "Magic flying carpet . . . fly out this bedroom window!"

VROOM! VROOM!

Marigold just managed to climb aboard before they zoomed out the window.

Winnie shouted into the starry night. "WHEE-E-E-E!"

Marigold held on to the sides of the carpet with every ounce of her strength and wished for the hundredth time that she'd figured out how to fly.

The carpet circled Winnie's house, which was several stories high and sat atop a tall lonely mountain with just a full moon to keep it company. The only other sign of life came from off in the distance, where a wisp of smoke drifted out from the chimney of a small house.

They were traveling at a good clip. Several petals flew off Marigold's head. Her eyes teared, and her arms ached from holding on so tightly to the magic flying carpet, but she had only one thing on her mind: Bramblycrumbly. Exactly how long did she have, she wondered, to make friends with this girl?

"Winnie?" Marigold yelled over the wind. "Would you

happen to know about what time you'll be turning nine tomorrow?"

"Who cares?" Winnie yelled back.

They flew down, down, down, past lots of little stores, a park, and some houses. Thankfully the carpet took on a more sensible speed as it headed out of town. Marigold ventured a look below, where a huge dark, scary-looking forest—thick with trees—loomed along the horizon. A chill ran up her spine because it looked like Spookety Forest!

Marigold tried again. "Could you give me an estimate of what time you'll turn nine? Like seven a.m.? Or twelve noon?"

"Who knows!" Winnie yelled. She looked like she was having the time of her life.

Marigold worried. What if this girl turned nine at 12:01 or 12:02? How much time would that leave for her to complete the Invis-O-Friend spell? It couldn't be more than a few hours till midnight. Could she make friends with the most unfriendly girl in town by then?

The magic flying carpet swooped over the tops of trees, and Winnie spotted something. "Look, there's a boy down there!" She leaned precariously over the side of the carpet. "Maybe he's seen my magic wand—I'm going to find out." Winnie ordered the carpet to land. "And I'll make sure he doesn't see my magic flying carpet. No way is some dopey boy going to take it away from me like that stupid shadow took my wand!"

The carpet obeyed. It spiraled to earth and landed behind some bushes. Winnie rolled it up and put it under one arm. She peeked over the foliage at the boy, who paced in front of a wrought iron gate. Marigold could see it was exactly the same as the entrance to Spookety Forest in Bramblycrumbly. "Seepage!" she whispered for the second time that night. It had happened again!

Winnie peered over the bush, sizing up the boy. "I don't like the looks of him one little bit."

Marigold thought just the opposite. "I'll bet he's nice."

"I'll bet he stinks." Winnie stepped out from behind the bushes.

The boy looked startled.

"What's your name?" she barked.

"I'm Norman." He had bright red hair and freckles. His ears stuck out and so did his two front teeth. He tilted his head. "Hey, aren't you the most unfriendly girl in town, called Winifred or something?"

"Winnie," she snapped.

Marigold stood beside Winnie. "Ask him what time it is."

Winnie glanced at Marigold. "What is it with you and the time?"

"Who are you talking to?" Norman asked.

"None of your beeswax," Winnie replied. "What time is it?"

Norman looked at his watch. "It's eight thirty-three."

Marigold calculated that this left her at least three hours and twenty-seven minutes to complete the spell or else Bramblycrumbly might be toast.

Winnie folded her arms. "What are you doing here?" she asked suspiciously.

"I'm looking for my dog," Norman replied. "He ran off into that forest— Are you wearing your pajamas under that cape?"

"I was going to bed early because tomorrow is my birthday and I need my rest. I'm having a fabulous birthday party." Winnie narrowed her eyes. "And *you're* not invited."

The boy shrugged. "That's okay," he said good-naturedly.

Winnie scowled. "So, if you're looking for your dog, what are you standing here for?"

"I just saw a ghost in those woods!" Norman pointed his chin at the ominous wall of trees behind him and shuddered.

Winnie's eyes lit up. "Which way did he go?"

"Who? The ghost? Or Meatball?" Norman asked.

"Who's Meatball?" Winnie huffed.

"My dog," Norman said.

Winnie rolled her eyes. "Stupid name for a dog," she said under her breath as she headed for the entrance to the forest.

"Aren't you afraid of ghosts?" Norman called after her.

"Nope," Winnie replied. She opened the gate. Marigold thought it creaked as eerily in the Human World as it had in Bramblycrumbly.

Winnie marched off into the forest, calling for the shadow boy to give her back her wand. Norman followed, calling for his dog, Meatball. Marigold entered behind them into the gloom, worrying. With every step she repeated the words from the Invis-O-Friend Spell: *laughter, joy, advice,*

sorrow . . . laughter, joy, advice, sorrow—all the things she'd have to share with a human who'd never had a friend in her entire life, and Marigold only had a little over three hours to do this. It seemed impossible. She squinted into the dark forest and saw ghosts weaving their way in and out of trees. They spotted Winnie right away and dive-bombed her, trying to grab her bag of candy.

"Why, you!" Winnie windmilled her arms. "I ought to knock your blocks off!"

It wasn't going to be easy to get Winnie to share anything with Marigold, but at least Marigold could share some advice with Winnie. "Winnie, why don't you try being friendly and just give them a piece?"

"Give them my candy?" Winnie said, appalled at even the thought. "I'll give them a knuckle sandwich!" The girl made a fist and shook it at the ghost children.

Norman hid behind a tree. "Um, I don't think you should make them mad."

Marigold looked around frantically for the smallest flicker or movement, some indication that the shadow boy was near. She strained her eyes to see the least bit of sparkle from her magic wand. Sure enough, in the shade of a giant rhododendron was a telltale glint. She took some uncertain steps toward what she thought might be the shadow boy's hiding place, just like she had only hours ago when she and Lightning had first spotted him in Spookety Forest. Sure enough, there he was! They locked eyes. His were soft and warm. She was positive that, in that moment, all he wanted was to be friends and give her back her wand. Marigold slowly reached for it. The next moment, the ghost children shouted for help, and the shadow boy slipped away into the brush.

"Marigold Star! The Winnie won't give us her candy!"

Marigold watched as Winnie teased the ghosts. She took candy from the bag, only to pop it into her own mouth. "MMMMM, delicious!" She dangled the bag in front of them. When they tried to grab it, she pulled it out of reach. She held the bag at arm's length to do the same trick again, but then without warning, a long dog with short legs and a fuzzy snout bounded over a bush onto the trail. He grabbed Winnie's bag of candy and raced into the forest with it.

"Give me back my candy!" Winnie sputtered.

"Meatball!" Norman yelled.

They took off in hot pursuit.

Marigold was about to run after all three of them when her star started to blink.

"Not again!" She stood frozen in place, unable to do anything but look at the flashing light from the star.

Off. On. Off. On. Off. On.

Marigold closed her eyes, wishing it away. By the time she opened them and looked around, Meatball, Winnie, and Norman were gone.

She walked unsurely down the path deeper into the forest, scolding herself. What had she been thinking to take her eyes off Winnie? "Hello?" Marigold called in a small voice. She looked left. She looked right. She walked a little farther. "Winnie?" she said a little louder. All the while her star blinked.

"Oh! Why does this have to happen now?" She could feel herself start to panic. *What if I can't find Winnie? How will I ever make friends with her? What time is it?* Her mind was spinning and she could barely think straight.

"Winnie! Where are you?" Marigold cried out, but there was no one there.

She leaned against a tree. She had lost her magic wand, and now she had lost the other thing that could keep Bramblycrumbly from certain disaster: Winnie! Awful thoughts marched through her mind, one after the other, of brambles growing like wildfire over Baddie's shack, Mrs. Moon's nest, and Bob's woodpiles—not to mention her own home in the shape of a teapot. "It would all be my fault! I have to find Winnie! I have to find her now!"

Her hand reached into her pocket where she had shoved Granny's spell book, desperate for any kind of help it might offer. Once again it opened to the fateful Invis-O-Friend Spell, and that's when Marigold had an idea! If she repeated the spell—the same one that had gotten her into Winnie's room in the first place—wouldn't it take her right back to Winnie, "the most friendless of friends"? Of course—it was so simple! Why hadn't she thought of this right away?

Marigold quickly chanted, "Izzable, dizzable, make me invisible to all but one. Send me to the most friendless of friends—unless I've never been a friend before."

She closed her eyes like she was supposed to.

But when Marigold opened them, Winnie was not there.

8

LENNY

There were comic books. Thousands of comic books. Stacks upon crooked stacks of them reaching upward to a ceiling. A narrow aisle between stacks zigzagged its way to the far corner of a room where only one light glowed over a little bed littered with banana peels, candy wrappers, and several boxes of cookies. On the bed sat a boy, his eyes wide, his mouth gaping open in surprise. "Awesome," he whispered. "I always knew this would happen."

The boy climbed off his bed and approached Marigold with wonder. He was short and round with dark curly hair and thick glasses. He wore sweatpants and a hoodie with spots down the front. He stood before her and pointed to himself with his thumb. "I'm Lenny."

"I'm Marigold Star," she replied.

"Where are you from?" he asked. Without giving Marigold a chance to answer, he held up his hands and said, "Wait, don't tell me—you've come from an alien world, from a technologically advanced species, right? Or no—maybe you came from a secluded island in the middle of a vast ocean?"

Before he thought up another place she could have come from, Marigold quickly answered, "I'm from Bramblycrumbly."

"Whoa." Lenny took several steps back and gazed at Marigold, spellbound.

Marigold smiled at him and was glad that at least he seemed friendly. Her star had stopped blinking as well, but as far as she could tell, those were the only two good things about her situation. How had she ended up here? Where was she? More important, where were Winnie and her magic wand? She had to make friends with the unpleasant girl to complete the spell and find her magic wand. If she failed to do both, it was going to be goodbye, Bramblycrumbly! "I'm sorry. I've landed in the wrong place—this is a huge mistake."

He seemed not to hear and instead knelt on one knee, lowered his head, and put his hand over his heart. "I am your lowly servant, ready to do your bidding."

Marigold tilted her head. "My what?"

Lenny looked up. "Your bidding—your bidding, you know, like, I'll do whatever you want me to do." He waited expectantly, but when Marigold didn't answer, he said, "No? Okay, scratch that. I've got a better idea." He stood and then bowed deeply. "I am your trusty sidekick, ready to follow you on your heroic journey and stick by your side no matter what while we both change the world and you take all the credit."

"What are you talking about?" Marigold was completely flummoxed by this strange boy.

"I'm your faithful sidekick." Lenny pointed to himself again and grinned broadly. "All superheroes have one."

Marigold shook her head. She was not a hero of any kind—super or otherwise—and she told the boy this.

Lenny disagreed. "You *are* a superhero."

"Oh no, I'm *not*," she said emphatically.

"Oh yes, you *are!*" he insisted. "I should know. I've read every single one of these comic books about a million times. And they're all about superheroes"—he pointed to Marigold— "like *you*." The boy nodded to himself as if to confirm the idea. "You've come to life straight out of my imagination," he murmured. "I always knew this would happen." He jumped up and down and clapped his hands, but a moment later he became somber.

"What?" Marigold asked.

"It's just that . . ." Lenny lowered his eyes; he bit his lip. "I always thought you'd have, like, a cool cape . . . or a better costume . . . or . . . hair."

"It's a flower," Marigold pointed out.

"Right!" Lenny said excitedly. "Because when you were a baby, you ate a radioactive flower by mistake! Do you have a secret weapon?"

"I have a magic power," Marigold said.

"Great! What is it?" Lenny asked.

"That's my problem—I don't know," Marigold replied.

The boy gave a dismissive wave of his hand and went back to the corner of his room. "It's not a problem—it happens all the time with superheroes. They, like, hardly ever know what their superpower is in the beginning."

Marigold barely heard a word the boy said. She had to

find Winnie—and her wand! "Lenny, what time is it?" she asked anxiously.

"Five minutes after nine," he said eagerly. "Why?"

Marigold made the calculation. "That only leaves two hours and fifty-five minutes."

"Wow! Midnight, right?" Lenny said excitedly. "What happens? Do you turn into something cool? Like a robot or . . . Wait—does your archenemy destroy the world at midnight unless you stop him?"

"I don't have an archenemy." Marigold hurried toward the door. "I just have to go find Winnie—now!"

Lenny grabbed his sneakers. "Can I come?"

"I don't think that's such a good idea." Marigold turned to leave, but a small girl wearing pajamas stood blocking the doorway.

Lenny yanked on some socks. "Tell Mom I'm going out."

"But you never go out," the little girl said.

"Well, I am now." He furiously laced up his sneakers. "I'm moving out of the known conventional safety of my bedroom to answer a call to adventure to serve Marigold Star on her heroic journey."

The girl wrinkled her nose. "Who's Marigold Star?"

"Her." Lenny pointed at Marigold.

"Who?" the girl said, looking all around the room.

Lenny plucked a knit cap off a hook on the wall. "Oh, that's right—you can't see her because she's not real."

"I am too real." Marigold scooted around the little girl, whom she assumed was Lenny's sister.

"Yeah, but only to me." Lenny pushed past her as well, but when he reached the front door, he stopped. "Um . . . there's only one thing." He bit a fingernail. "I don't like to go outside."

"Why not?" Marigold asked.

Lenny frowned. "Because there are people. Then again, we probably won't be running into any of them—we'll probably be taking your rocket ship, right?"

Marigold shook her head. "No."

Lenny said hopefully, "Or your Marigold Super-Starmobile?"

"Uh-uh," Marigold said.

"Or you'll bestow your magic flying powers onto me and we'll both fly?" Lenny asked.

"I can't fly," Marigold admitted.

"Wait." Lenny held up one finger. "Let me guess. It's because you're afraid, right?"

"How did you know?" Marigold said, surprised.

"It's totally normal." He pulled the knit cap down over his ears. "You're just having a temporary lapse of self-confidence." He rolled his eyes. "It happens to, like, every single superhero there's ever been. But don't worry, that's where I come in."

"It is?" Marigold was astounded.

"Sure." He stepped outside. "It's practically the whole reason why they invented sidekicks."

It was a beautiful night with a full moon. Lenny walked next to Marigold down the street. "As we set off on our quest, I have just one question, sir: who's Winnie?"

"Winnie is the most unfriendly girl in her town," Marigold replied. "In fact, she doesn't have a single friend—can you imagine?"

"Yeah— I mean, no. That's crazy, not having even a *single* friend." Lenny laughed nervously.

"It's so easy to make friends. I can't imagine not having even a single one!" Marigold exclaimed.

"Yeah, me either." Lenny mumbled, "Except maybe if a

kid moved to, like, a new neighborhood. They might not have a single friend. . . ."

Marigold shrugged. "But then all they'd have to do is make new friends!"

"New friends—exactly." Lenny nodded. "But why do you need to find Winnie?"

Marigold explained, "I was trying to learn how to become invisible, and I did this spell called the Invis-O-Friend Spell and somehow ended up in Winnie's room, then—"

Lenny interrupted, "When was the last time you saw Winnie, sir?"

"About half an hour ago—and you don't have to call me 'sir,'" Marigold said.

"Okay, Captain." Lenny made a little salute.

"You don't have to call me 'Captain' either." Marigold didn't want to hurt Lenny's feelings, but she had to convince him that she wasn't a superhero!

"How about boss?" he asked.

"How about just calling me Marigold?" She smiled and continued. "So, Winnie had my magic wand—"

"Hold it. Back up." Lenny put his hands on top of his head, as if it might explode otherwise. "Don't you know that you're *never* supposed to give your magic wand to someone else?"

"How do you know that?" Marigold had heard that magic wands didn't exist in the Human World.

Lenny stared at the ground, his eyes wide with the obviousness of the answer. "It's practically superhero rule number one!"

Marigold gave him a sidelong glance. "Well, to make matters worse, actually, Super Scary Shadow Boy has it now, and—"

Lenny stopped dead in his tracks. "Super Scary Shadow Boy? Are you kidding me? I *love* Super Scary Shadow Boy!" He instantly produced a comic book from his back pocket to show her. "That's what I was just reading before you appeared! Look!"

A queasy feeling rose in Marigold's stomach. On the cover of Lenny's comic book, it practically screamed: **"IN A NEVER-ENDING BATTLE, SUPER SCARY SHADOW BOY DEFENDS GHOSTS THE WORLD OVER!"** There was a picture of a small shadowy figure with claws and fangs and a pointy tail cast onto the rocky wall of a cave. She flipped through the pages to see that the comic was identical to the story she had told the ghost children. The words from Granny's spell book instantly came to mind: "Seepage: When characters, places, and/or objects spontaneously appear in a world other than their own."

Lenny bobbed up and down with nervous energy. "We have to find Super Scary Shadow Boy right away! We have to get your magic wand back! I mean, he's Super Scary Shadow Boy! What if he uses it to make an army of super ghosts? What if they wage a ruthless war against all mankind? What if they destroy the *world*?" Lenny hurried off, talking to himself. "That would be so *awesome*."

"You don't know the full story, Lenny!" Marigold ran after the boy. "If I don't find Winnie and make friends with her before midnight *and* if I don't find my wand by then, Bramblycrumbly will crumble and turn to brambles."

"Well, that would be awful," Lenny said. "But also kind of cool."

Marigold gave him a harsh look.

Lenny softened. "Look, it's going to be all right, Marigold. All we have to do is find Super Scary Shadow Boy, get your wand back, and wish for Winnie to appear. Simple. Super

Scary Shadow Boy is probably in Spookety Forest playing Candy Land in his creepy dark cave this very minute—he loves Candy Land."

Lenny took off at a run.

"Wait!" Marigold called. "Where are you going?"

"To find Spookety Forest!" he called over his shoulder. "It's not safe, Marigold—but danger is what superheroes thrive on!"

"But I'm not a superhero!" Marigold yelled. She chased after the boy for several blocks. The houses on each street became shabbier. Roofs sagged, weeds grew high in yards, and windows were boarded up. She didn't want to lose Lenny too and ran to catch up. Just up ahead, he came to a halt.

"There!" Lenny pointed at a wrought iron gate surrounded by brambles. Marigold recognized the familiar landmark. Once again here was Spookety Forest.

9

TRIALS AND ORDEALS

Lenny zipped through the gate.

Marigold followed. They ran under the canopy of trees into the moonlit world that she had come to know so well. Lenny walked alongside her, trying to be helpful. "All we have to do is find the ghosts, and they'll know exactly where Super Scary Shadow Boy is. *And* Spookety Forest is *loaded* with them. Watch this!" He dipped into his pocket and pulled out a handful of jelly beans. "Here, ghosts! Come and get it, guys!"

Sure enough, a moment later several ghosts floated quickly toward them.

"Hello, ghosts. I'm Lenny, and—"

They knocked the jelly beans out of Lenny's hand and

swarmed around Marigold. "Help, Marigold Star!" they cried.

"Where have you been?" said one.

"We've been looking all over for you!" said another.

"Where is Winnie?" Marigold asked urgently.

"Super Scary Shadow Boy has her," said a third ghost. "He'll never let her go!"

The ghosts started to moan, and Marigold tried to console them. "Don't worry, I'm sure he won't harm Winnie."

They flew wildly about, and their voices echoed up into the trees. "We don't care about her!"

"What, then?" Marigold asked.

"He says he's going to make us invisible if we're not his friends," one ghost said.

"He makes us play Candy Land with him—in his super scary dark cave!" said another.

"He thinks he's a superhero!" They all chimed in.

"He is!" Lenny said, and they thumped him on the head. "Stop that!" Lenny shouted, but they paid no attention.

"Marigold Star! He's too scary! We don't want to be friends with a shadow boy! You have to come and tell him to stop making us play Candy Land. We hate Candy Land.

But we're too afraid not to play, because if we don't, he'll make us invisible!" The ghosts flew away. "Come with us, Marigold Star!" they implored.

"To where?" she shouted. "Where is Super Scary Shadow Boy?"

"Spookety Cave!" They flew off through the trees into the dark forest.

"But you know I can't fly! Send the ghost train!" Marigold watched with dismay as they disappeared.

Lenny's eyes glittered with excitement. "What's the ghost train?"

"It's the only fast way to Spookety Cave, but you never know when one will arrive, and the ghosts are so upset, I'm not sure they'll be able to get one to come now." Marigold's shoulders sagged. Even the petals on her head drooped. She pushed them out of her eyes, but they fell right back. "Spookety Cave is way on the other side of the forest. It'll be well past midnight by the time we walk there. What am I going to do? I just feel like giving up, Lenny!" Marigold started to cry; it seemed like everything was conspiring against her.

Lenny shook his head. "You can't give up now—are you

kidding? This is the best part."

"What do you mean, 'the best part'?" Marigold sniffed.

"Trials and ordeals, Marigold." Lenny spoke in a low, mysterious voice. "You can't be a superhero without them.

"Lenny, how many times do I have to tell you I'm not a superhero!" Marigold cried with frustration.

"Look, it's only through overcoming trials and ordeals that the ordinary person becomes strong enough to become a superhero. Without them you'll never know the power you possess!"

Marigold hoped that what Lenny had just said didn't apply to powers obtained through the Invis-O-Friend Spell—she was terrible at trials and ordeals! Like Spelling Test Day at school, when everyone had to pick three spells and learn them by the end of the day. Marigold had failed her first one so miserably and had come to dread Spelling Test Day so much that she had started to feign illness. But now she had to get her wand back and find Winnie before the girl turned nine and make friends with her. All of Bramblycrumbly depended on it—she couldn't pretend she had a stomachache! "If only I could fly!" Marigold crouched and said the Flying Spell: "Spoket! Spoket!

Magic poket! Fly!" At the same time, she flung her arms and leaped.

Thud. She landed in the dirt. "I'm hopeless," she moaned.

Lenny helped her up. "No, you're not—your timing is just off."

"My timing?" She was doubtful.

"Yes, it's all about timing," Lenny replied. "I know exactly what you're doing wrong. Right as you say the word 'fly,' you need to spring in the air."

Marigold had no idea what he was talking about.

"You're waiting too long . . . you're leaping too late . . . you're not following through . . . you're stopping yourself."

"How?" Marigold was interested to know.

"After you say 'poket,' you need to take a deep breath, exhale hard, fling your arms in the air, and leap on the word 'fly.'"

"It sounds complicated," Marigold said.

"It's really not—it's just a matter of timing."

"But I'm afraid," Marigold said.

"Of what?"

"It's so high up in the air and dangerous." She shuddered.

"But it's so fun! I wish I could fly!" Lenny held out his

arms and ran in a circle. "Soaring through the clouds—think of all the places you could get to quickly . . . um, like now."

Marigold gritted her teeth and tried again. "Spoket! Spoket! Magic poket! Fly!"

Thud! She landed in the dirt again. She sat there not moving, trying to think of how she was going to get to Spookety Cave. It certainly wouldn't be by flying.

"What time is it now, Lenny?" she asked.

"Nine thirty-five," he answered way too cheerfully.

Lenny had such unwavering belief in her, but as far as Marigold could tell, her options were fading fast. "I'm going to have to call Big Flying Bird," she muttered, thinking at least Seepage was good for something.

"See? I knew you'd come up with an idea!" Lenny exclaimed.

"Don't get too excited," Marigold said. "He's very sensitive and gets mad at the least little thing. He's mad at me right now because my dragon said he was as big as an elephant."

"Is he?" Lenny asked.

"Yes, but he wishes he were only the size of a parrot—like

all his brothers and sisters." Marigold stood, readying herself to say the spell. She had to get it right for once. "Stand back," she warned. "And whatever you do—don't call him 'big.'" She took a deep breath and said: "Twinkle, twinkle, Big Flying Bird. Come to me with these few words, I wish I may, I wish I might, have the bird I wish tonight!"

Much to her shock and amazement, she got it right. Before them stood the magnificent bird. His golden legs and pointy beak gleamed in the half-light. His inky-black and snow-white feathers were perfectly groomed. The majestic plume on the top of his head looked more regal than ever. He was still as big as an elephant.

Lenny stared, unable to speak for a moment.

"Who's that?" The bird eyed the boy suspiciously.

"This is my friend Lenny," Marigold replied.

"Humph." He narrowed his eyes. "All I can say is that you have terrible taste in friends. First that awful excuse for a dragon, now this oddly *human*-looking Lenny." Before Marigold could answer, the bird cocked his head. "Does this plume make me look big?"

"N-No—not at all," Marigold stammered.

The bird ruffled his feathers. "So, what's with the blinking star still—I thought you were going to Granny's to fix that?"

Marigold raised her eyes to see, and sure enough, the bird was right. "Not again!" She groaned.

"Cool!" Lenny exclaimed. "I'll bet it means your archenemy is near."

Marigold gave the boy a withering look.

"I told you, I'm very sensitive to light—make it stop!" The bird stamped his foot.

"I can't make it stop," Marigold wailed.

The bird's cheeks turned bright red. "I'm very sorry, but I can't work under these conditions." He flapped his wings, and feathers filled the air. "No one said anything about a blinking star—and don't tell me I'm too sensitive!"

"Sensitive? We would never say that." Marigold smoothed his feathers with her hand. "Right, Lenny?"

"Sensitive? You? Never!" Lenny tried to sound convincing. "And might I say that you are looking especially *small* today."

"Really?" the bird said with delighted surprise.

Lenny nodded. "Almost as small as a *parrot*."

"Do you really think so?" the bird asked hopefully.

"I really think so," Lenny replied with a straight face.

The bird was all smiles. "Well, thank you," he said, pleased.

Marigold and Lenny exchanged relieved glances.

"Where to?" the bird asked politely.

"Could you take us to Spookety Cave?" Marigold asked.

The bird lowered himself, and Lenny climbed onto his back, where two little seats had been strapped on. As soon as they were seated, Big Flying Bird took off at a run, his strides growing larger with each step until he pushed off the ground with a grunt and they were airborne.

"Boy, he really is sensitive," Lenny said in a low voice.

Marigold nodded. "We're going to have to be careful about what we say."

Lenny covered his mouth with his hand. "This bird sure isn't very fast." It was true.

They put-putted along at about the speed of a flying turtle.

"We'll never get to Winnie at this rate," Marigold fretted. "What time is it now, Lenny?"

"Nine fifty," he reported.

"Two hours and ten minutes! Oh!" Marigold wrung her hands. "Please hurry, bird," she murmured, though she didn't dare say it too loud for fear of hurting his feelings. How was she ever going to find Winnie and make friends with the most unfriendly girl in town in such a short amount of time? She glanced at Lenny to see he had a huge grin plastered across his face, like he was enjoying himself immensely. "You don't seem very worried," Marigold remarked.

"Because I know you'll eventually find Winnie, make friends, and save Bramblycrumbly," Lenny replied.

Marigold furrowed her brow. Her heart thudded uncontrollably in her chest. So many things had gone wrong—how could Lenny still be so unconcerned? "I'm glad you have so much faith in me, Lenny—but I'm not so sure."

"I am!" Lenny said confidently. "In fact, I know for certain you're even going to learn to fly before this night is up."

Marigold was doubtful.

Lenny explained, "For example, what if right now Big Flying Bird suddenly vanished? You'd know that I was going to be squashed on the ground, and out of a selfless desire to save my life, you would totally forget that you can't fly. Your superhero super-abilities would take over—because of course you've been able to fly all along, you just didn't know it, and voila, you're flying!"

"That's crazy, Lenny!" Marigold exclaimed. "I don't have any superhero super-abilities, and—I can't fly!"

Lenny suddenly had a funny look on his face. "Tell the truth, Marigold." He spoke in a loud voice. "That plume on Big Flying Bird really does make him look big."

The bird slowed. "What?"

"I said," Lenny answered, "Big Flying Bird looks big."

"No—he didn't mean it!" Marigold cried.

"Yes, I did," Lenny said. "It's plain to see he's as big as an elephant."

"A-as big as an e-elephant?" the bird sputtered.

"Yeah, and I think you're too sensitive," Lenny added.

"Then fly yourself around, kid!" the bird said.

Poof! He vanished.

Marigold and Lenny locked eyes as they hovered in the air for a split second. Then they were falling like two bags of cement. Lenny took Marigold's hand. "Fly, Marigold! Don't be afraid!"

"Spoket! Spoket! Magic poket!" Marigold said. But they kept right on falling. "Fly!" she repeated. "Fly! Fly! Fly!" she screamed. The wind whistled in her ears as they continued to fall.

Oh, if only she were back in Bramblycrumbly with Lightning or with Granny Cabbage! If only she and Lenny were anywhere but here right now, about to be squashed on the ground! In fact, she'd never needed to be somewhere else more than she did right now. The ground came roaring at Marigold with tremendous speed. Marigold squeezed Lenny's hand with all her might. The spell had sent her somewhere else twice tonight—maybe it would do it again now. . . . "Izzable dizzable, make me invisible to all but one. Send me to the most friendless of friends—unless I've never been a friend before." She braced herself . . . she clenched her teeth . . . she closed her eyes.

BAM!

10

PRISCILLA

"It stopped," Lenny said.

Marigold opened her eyes to see him kneeling over her. She was lying beside a large fir tree, and all around her was an open grassy area.

"Your star—it stopped blinking," Lenny repeated. "And we didn't both get squashed on the ground either. We're alive!"

"Yay," Marigold said weakly. There was little to be cheerful about. She was further away than ever from finding Winnie and completing the Invis-O-Friend Spell or from getting her magic wand back, for that matter. Marigold rose onto her elbows and looked around.

"We're not even in Spookety Forest anymore!" Marigold groaned.

"We're in a park," Lenny said. "You know—baseball . . . soccer?"

They had parks in Bramblycrumbly but for games like tiddlytag and wumble-dob—games that Marigold never played because they involved flying.

She stood and turned slowly in a circle, but nothing looked familiar to her. "We have to get back to Spookety Forest, Lenny! What time is it now?"

"Five after ten." He ducked under the branches of the fir tree. "Quick—hide!"

Sure enough, a short distance away in a picnic area, Marigold could just make out the form of someone sitting under a table. She squinted. "I wonder what they're doing there all by themselves in the dark."

"Shhhh," Lenny hissed. "It might be your archenemy . . . or an evil entity!"

"I already told you, I don't have an archenemy," Marigold said. "Come on, let's go see who it is."

Lenny crouched even lower. "You go—I've got your back."

Marigold started off. It was a short walk, and she called as soon as she was near. These were not the greatest circumstances for making friends, and the call might have startled anyone who somehow found themselves under a picnic table, alone in the dark. When she was close enough, Marigold introduced herself in her usual friendly manner, which always put others at ease. She extended her hand. "Hi, I'm Marigold Star."

A girl with a large orange cat on her lap took Marigold's hand and replied, "I'm Priscilla." She looked to be about Marigold's age. She had straight, black, chin-length hair with bangs, and she was wearing a silver puffy jacket. The cat meowed mournfully, and Priscilla introduced him. "This is Boing-Boing."

Marigold patted the cat's head.

The girl sniffed. Her eyes and nose were red, and a large tear rolled down her cheek.

Marigold had a soft heart and could never stand to see anyone unhappy—not even the occasional ant that managed to become separated from his family (she'd always take great pains to reunite him with his colony). She immediately felt sorry for Priscilla and offered her a piece of candy. Priscilla asked Marigold if she wanted to come under the table and sit with her for a while, and she scooted over to make room. While it was true that Marigold was in

a terrible hurry—what with it being five after ten and there only being an hour and fifty-five minutes left to find her wand and Winnie and complete the spell to auto-reverse the obvious Seepage that had taken place—she just had to keep this lonely girl company, if only for a short while.

Priscilla dried her tears. "I like your star."

"Everyone says it's a sure sign I'm marked for greatness, but I'm not great at anything," Marigold replied. "In fact, lately, I've made a perfect mess of things."

"Well, I'm sure glad you're here." Priscilla blew her nose. "My best friend moved away last year. That's when I got Boing-Boing." There was a slight catch in her voice that was plain to hear the girl tried to control.

Marigold patted Priscilla's shoulder and offered her another piece of candy. "So, what are you doing here?"

Priscilla hiccupped. "I-It's just not the s-same at home anymore."

"Baby sister, right?" Marigold said knowingly.

"Brother." Priscilla's cat meowed. "And the worst part is that he's allergic, and my parents said we have to get rid of him."

"Your brother?" Marigold asked.

"I wish," Priscilla said. "No, my cat." Priscilla shook her head and began with fresh tears.

"That's awful!" Marigold covered her face with her hands and felt like crying too, because she couldn't imagine having to give up Lightning.

Priscilla bent her head to look the cat straight in the eyes. "We're going to live here for the time being, right, Boing-Boing?" The cat answered with a plaintive meow.

Marigold pressed her lips together. "I don't blame you one bit. In fact, I have a baby sister, and I was thinking no one would even miss me if I went off and lived in the forest with my pet!"

"Dog?" Priscilla asked.

"No, dragon," Marigold replied.

"Better yet." Priscilla kissed the top of her cat's head, and he purred.

Marigold marveled at how much alike she and Priscilla were. She pushed an old paper cup out of the way and leaned to one side to move the top from a ketchup bottle that she'd been sitting on. "I think I can find you a better place than this—maybe a shack under a bridge or a nice little cottage in the woods."

"Do you really know of nice little cottages in the woods?" Priscilla asked, and for the first time a hopeful smile crossed her lips.

"Loads." Marigold pointed to the fir tree. "My friend Lenny is right over there, and we can both help you look."

Priscilla brightened.

Lenny wasn't as excited. He peeked out from under the branches of the fir tree. "Can she see you?"

Indeed, she could! Marigold had completely forgotten, and now she wondered why it was that Winnie and Lenny and Priscilla could see her but Winnie's mother, Norman, and Lenny's little sister couldn't. She thought about the spell—"Make me invisible to all but one"—but Marigold was invisible to all but three! Why?

"She can see me plain as the nose on your face!" Marigold said. "Her parents are making her get rid of her cat."

"So?" Lenny said.

"So, she needs a new place to live," Marigold answered.

Lenny crawled out from under the tree. He stood up and folded his arms. He looked angry. "This is *not* the way it's supposed to be. You're supposed to be looking for Winnie and your magic wand. I'm supposed to be helping you discover your magic power and restoring your confidence so that you can fly. I'm your trusty sidekick, *remember, hello*?"

"You're not my sidekick, Lenny," Marigold said gently.

"So now this Priscilla kid is?" He closed his eyes and shook his head. "N-O. NO. A superhero can't change sidekicks in the middle of the story. It's the rules!" He walked away. "I'm going home!" he called over his shoulder.

"Lenny! You don't even know where you are!" Marigold shouted. "Plus, I didn't say Priscilla was my sidekick!"

Lenny stopped. "She's not your sidekick?" he asked hopefully.

"No!" Marigold exclaimed.

Lenny considered this for a moment. "Wait a minute." He smacked his forehead with the heal of his hand. "She's your helpful servant, right?"

"No," Marigold replied.

"Of course!" he said excitedly. "She's an evil entity!"

"Nope," Marigold answered.

"Mentor?" His shoulders sagged.

Marigold shook her head.

"Guardian at the gate?" His voice rose an octave.

"No. NO. *NO!*" Marigold stamped her foot.

Lenny's eyes grew large with fear. "Well, then, w-who is s-she?"

Marigold shrugged. "She's just a girl."

"A girl," Lenny said as if it was the worst of all possibilities. "You. Mean. A. *Real*. Girl?"

"A real girl," Marigold replied.

Right on cue they both could see Priscilla walking toward them. Lenny dived back under the fir tree.

Marigold's mouth dropped open. Lenny had walked straight into a dark, scary, ghost-filled forest all by himself; had climbed onto the back of Big Flying Bird, who had vanished right out from under him; and had almost gotten himself squashed on the ground without showing the least bit of fear. She bent to get a closer look at the expression on his face. It just didn't make sense that he'd be scared of a mere girl. "You're not *afraid* of this girl, are you?"

Lenny bit his lip. "Not this girl specifically. . . ." His voice trailed off. "It's just that I don't like to talk to people or sit next to them or eat lunch with them or be with them in general."

126

"But you don't mind being with me," Marigold reminded him.

"Because I made you up," he whispered with impatience. And no matter how Marigold tried to explain that she was not "made up" and that she was as real as Priscilla, he refused to come out from under the fir tree.

"Lenny!" Marigold pleaded. She grabbed his hands and tried to pull him out physically, but Lenny wouldn't budge. "We can find Spookety Forest *and* help Priscilla find a nice little cottage in the woods too."

"And then will she leave?" he called from his hiding place.

"Then I'll leave," Priscilla said, for she was standing right next to Marigold by now.

"Good," Lenny muttered. He finally appeared, but his hood was up and all you could see was his nose.

Marigold, Priscilla, and Boing-Boing made their way across the ball fields, along with Lenny trailing behind. With Marigold's star to light the way, they found a path at the edge of the park that disappeared into some woods.

Lenny confirmed what Marigold already knew.

"FYI! This isn't Spookety Forest!" he shouted from a good ten feet back.

But whenever Marigold and Priscilla stopped for him to catch up, he stopped. It was dark, and Marigold was afraid that he would become separated the way Winnie had. "Come walk with us, Lenny!" Marigold kept calling to the boy. But when she'd turn to see where he was, he'd jump behind a bush.

Priscila was puzzled. "Why won't he walk with us?"

Marigold had given this some thought. She had known certain members of the Cabbage Family (some of whom were even her best friends) as well as a few of the Potato Family who rarely ventured outside. They spent their time reading and drawing wonderful pictures of places that they would never visit because they were too afraid to go out. Many of the trolls—though not Baddie, who was always very friendly—were this way as well. In fact, Marigold's mother had made many a house call to one or another of the Potatoes who'd actually taken root to their couch and had to be surgically removed! Still, no amount of cajoling or pleading for them to come out would make any difference. They were just too afraid of everyone except those they'd grown up with and seen every day. "Lenny is shy," Marigold finally concluded.

Priscilla understood. "Sometimes it's hard to make friends. Since mine moved away, I don't have a single one."

"You have no friends at all?" Marigold asked, surprised because Priscilla seemed so easy to talk to and so nice.

Priscilla hugged her cat. "Only Boing-Boing."

The words from the Invis-O-friend Spell echoed in Marigold's head: "invisible to all but the most friendless of friends." She was visible to Winnie, to Lenny, and now to Priscilla—and none of them had any friends! This had to mean that not only was Winnie her "visible friend," as the Invis-O-Friend Spell had referred to her, but so were Lenny and Priscilla!

Priscilla was speaking. "Do you really think we'll find a nice little cottage in these woods?"

"Yes," Marigold said confidently. In Bramblycrumbly nice little cottages could be found if you looked hard enough. "Where I come from, people leave their cottages in excellent shape for the next person to move into. It's considered polite and good luck."

"Where do you come from?" Priscilla asked.

"Bramblycrumbly." It gave Marigold the worst feeling to think of it crumbling if she failed to make friends with

Winnie and get her wand back from the shadow boy. It didn't matter that Priscilla and Lenny were "visible friends" because according to Granny's spell book in the Lost or Missing Wands section, under The Good News!, it stated that the only way to auto-reverse Seepage was to retrieve the missing magic wand and complete the Invis-O-Friend Spell with the visible friend from whom the spell had originated—which would be Winnie. Then and only then would things return to their proper worlds and Bramblycrumbly would be safe.

Marigold called back to Lenny, "What time is it?"

"Ten forty-five!" he shouted.

Marigold shook her head sadly and told Priscilla all that had happened up to the point where they met in the park. Priscilla listened with attention to Marigold's tale and asked just the right questions. Marigold felt more and more like she'd known this girl forever. Priscilla just automatically seemed to understand her—especially when Marigold talked about her star.

"I know exactly how you feel." Priscilla sympathized. "I'm supposedly 'gifted.'"

"What's 'gifted'?" All Marigold could think of were the

gifts of yarn she always brought to Baddie or the blueberry crumble that she always had for Granny.

Priscilla explained, "'Gifted' here just means that I did well on a test and that I should be really great at something someday."

Marigold understood. "Sort of like my star," she said.

"Exactly." Priscilla exhaled loudly. "My parents want to know what I'll be great at. They make me take all kinds of lessons, like piano, karate, chess, gymnastics, Chinese, golf, and ballroom dancing. They keep hoping that I'll be great at least in one of these, but so far I stink at everything."

They walked on in silence. Marigold hadn't heard of any of these lessons, but it sounded tiring to have to take so many. In any case, she couldn't believe she'd met someone—a human, no less—who finally understood her problem with her star.

"You might not be great at anything yet, Priscilla, but you're a great friend—and that's really important." Just saying these words made Marigold remember that Granny had said the same exact thing to her. She could see now what the old cabbage had meant.

Priscilla glanced at Marigold. "I wish I could go to Bramblycrumbly with you."

"Maybe you can!" Marigold explained Seepage and how she hoped that Spookety Forest was here the way it had been first in Winnie's neighborhood and then Lenny's.

"Can I come with you to help find Winnie?" Priscilla asked excitedly.

"I was hoping you'd say that!" Marigold laughed. "But what about your nice little cottage in the woods?"

"I'd much rather help you find Winnie and your magic wand," Priscilla replied. She was carrying Boing-Boing, who meowed, and Marigold took this as his vote to go find Winnie and the wand too.

11

GHOST TRAIN

Marigold was thrilled to have Priscilla and Boing-Boing along, and they all walked with renewed purpose through the woods. Lenny remained following from behind, making his presence known by shouting every now and then that they still hadn't found Spookety Forest.

This made Marigold worry. For the first time she wondered why Spookety Forest had appeared in Lenny's neighborhood, since Winnie could have been hundreds, if not thousands, of miles away from the boy. Marigold's heart began to flutter in her chest. Just now she had said the Invis-O-Friend Spell again, and she had no idea how far she had traveled from Lenny's to where they'd landed in the park. Why should she assume Spookety Forest was here in Priscilla's neighborhood as well? And what if it wasn't? She'd never find Winnie or her wand. All would be lost, crumbled, and covered in brambles.

Boing-Boing meowed plaintively. The four of them walked on and on in a fine mist, becoming wetter and colder by the minute. A fog settled on the ground, and they could barely see their feet. Marigold's mind raced trying to think of what to do. She was just about to reach for Granny's spell book to see if there was a way to get them out of this predicament when Priscilla said, "What's that?"

A few feet ahead, on the side of the path, was a wrought iron gate. Priscilla ran to it, and when she gave it a shove, it creaked just like the one in Bramblycrumbly. Priscilla peered off into the forest beyond the gate. "It looks like an entrance to something," she said excitedly.

Marigold heaved a sigh of relief. "It is."

They hurried under the canopy of trees and through the tunnel of foliage, their footfalls muffled by the soft moss. The path opened up to a glade, where beams of moonlight poked magically through the trees. Marigold halted to listen. There was a rumbling sound like thunder in the distance, then a whistle. *WOO! WOO!*

The sound got louder.

Priscilla ran to hide behind a tree, and her cat meowed with fear.

Lenny came running toward them. Marigold was happy to see him finally out in plain sight. "It's the ghost train, Lenny!" she exclaimed. He stood unmoving as the phantom vehicle neared. Marigold put Priscilla at ease. "Don't be scared. The ghost train is the fastest way to Spookety Cave, and the ghosts are friendly."

Shrouded in white, the train hovered above the ground, and tendrils of mist spiraled off the wheels. Milky fog swirled around their legs, climbing higher by the second, as if it would swallow them whole. The train stopped with a groaning and screeching of brakes before them, and a door silently slid open.

But no ghosts appeared. There were only voices.

"Help! Marigold Star!" said one.

"We're invisible!" said another.

"Super Scary Shadow Boy did this to us with his magic wand," said a third.

"Boo-hoo-hoo-hoo!" they wailed as a group.

Marigold knew the shadow boy had only done this to

the ghosts because they wouldn't be friends with him. She couldn't imagine what it must have been like for him to have everyone run in fright whenever he came around.

"Super Scary Shadow Boy won't hurt you—he just wants to be friends. Don't you remember the story I told you where he rescued the ghost child from the Human World?"

"We don't want to be friends. He's too scary!" The ghosts were all talking at once. "Come with us right away," ordered one.

"Tell him to turn us back!" called another.

"Does he still have Winnie?" Marigold asked anxiously.

"We already told you—he'll never let her go!" they cried.

The ghost conductor's voice could be heard: "All aboard for Winnie's Neighborhood. Winnie's Neighborhood, all aboard!"

WOO! WOO! The whistle blew. Lenny raced up the steps into the train.

Marigold and Priscilla climbed aboard as well. They followed Lenny through the mist that clung to the floor of the train. He walked through the car to the next one, and Marigold wondered when he was going to choose a seat.

"Hey, Lenny!" Priscilla called from behind. "How about this seat?"

Lenny ignored her. He passed to the next car.

"Lenny," Marigold said. "I think Priscilla is tired of carrying her cat. Let's just sit here." Lenny acted as if he hadn't heard her. He hurried all the way to the last car and Marigold finally knew why: he didn't want to have to talk to Priscilla and was hoping she would give up and take a seat in a car closer to the front. But Marigold kept her eye on Priscilla, making sure the girl didn't fall too far behind. She waited until she could see Priscilla and her cat entering the last car. Lenny sat down in the very last seat facing backward and Marigold slid in next to him.

"Phew," Lenny said in a low voice. "I thought we'd never get to this part, Marigold."

"What do you mean?" she asked.

"The part where we confront the villain—your archenemy! I can't wait!" He wiggled in his seat, barely able to contain his excitement.

"But Lenny . . ." Marigold closed her eyes and tried to stay calm. "I am *not* a superhero."

The boy would not be deterred. "We're on our way to

meet the Incredible Super Scary Shadow Boy and see his lair—and rescue Winnie!" Light glittered off his glasses, and his face beamed with joy, but a moment later his smile faded. Lenny immediately stopped talking.

Priscilla flopped into the seat across from Lenny. She still held the big orange cat. "Wow! I never knew that Boing-Boing was this heavy!"

Lenny didn't say a word.

Marigold tried to fill the awkward silence. "Can you believe that Priscilla has been carrying Boing-Boing all this time, Lenny?"

He mumbled something inaudible and turned to stare out the window.

WOO! WOO! The whistle sounded again. The dark mahogany paneling gleamed in the soft light, and the gold fringe on the curtains bounced as the train lurched forward.

A disembodied voice echoed down the aisle: "Tickets! Tickets please!"

Three tickets appeared before their eyes. They read: **"Destination: Winnie's Neighborhood,"** and a voice called out, "Next stop: Priscilla's Neighborhood!

Priscilla's Neighborhood, next stop!"

Boing-Boing meowed loudly. Priscilla patted his head and kissed his nose. Marigold was about to suggest something that Lenny could say to Priscilla when Priscilla glanced up from her cat and said, "Lenny?" He continued to stare out the window. "Lenny?" she repeated, but he still wouldn't look at her. Priscilla pressed on anyway. "I'm wondering . . . when the train came and the ghosts were all around us . . . why weren't you scared?"

"It's not just a train—it's a *ghost* train," he said under his breath.

"What?" Priscilla tilted her head because she hadn't understood a word of what he'd just said.

"A ghost train—G . . . H . . . O . . . S . . . T—ghost train." Lenny turned his shoulder to her and stared out the window.

Marigold intervened. "Lenny, tell Priscilla why you weren't scared when you heard all the ghosts."

With his eyes still focused out the window, Lenny shrugged. "It's just make-believe," he whispered so softly that he could barely be heard.

Priscilla leaned forward. "Make-believe?" she asked good-naturedly.

Lenny shrugged again. "It's all just made-up stuff, like in

all the stories . . . about superheroes. . . ." His voice trailed off.

Marigold stepped in again to help. "Lenny has read a lot about superheroes. How many comic books have you read, Lenny?"

Lenny shrugged yet again. "Like a million."

"Wow!" Priscilla said, impressed.

Lenny folded his arms and glanced nervously at Marigold. She quickly turned to Priscilla to keep the conversation going. "Do you like comic books?"

"I *love* comic books!" Priscilla said.

Lenny stole a look at the girl with the orange cat. "You do?"

"Mm-hm." She nodded.

Just then a ghost's voice announced, "Next stop: Priscilla's Neighborhood! Priscilla's Neighborhood, next stop!"

Neither Lenny nor Marigold said a word as the train pulled into the very park by the very picnic area in which they had just found Priscilla. The train came to a halt by the very table. Priscilla didn't budge.

"Don't you want to go home?" Lenny asked, his eyes averted.

Priscilla shook her head slightly and pressed her lips

together. This time it was Priscilla who seemed to feel shy. "I'd rather stay with Marigold and . . . you—i-if it's all right."

"Of course it's all right!" Marigold exclaimed. "Right, Lenny?"

Lenny didn't say—he looked out the window—but a little smile flickered across his lips.

"Next stop: Lenny's Neighborhood! Lenny's Neighborhood, next stop!" the ghost conductor shouted. The train started up with them for the second time that night. They chugged along slowly and rolled to a stop only a few moments later. Marigold could see they were right in front of Lenny's house.

Priscilla craned her neck to look out the window. "That's a nice house—is it yours, Lenny?" she asked.

"Yes," Lenny said, but he made no move to leave either.

"All out for Lenny's Neighborhood!" the conductor called.

Lenny grinned and held up his ticket. "I'm headed to Winnie's Neighborhood."

Priscilla held up hers. "Me too." As the train started up for the third time, she had a mysterious smile on her face.

Marigold felt encouraged. *Maybe Lenny and Priscilla could be friends after all*, she thought. She had to keep them talking. "Priscilla, Lenny has a little sister just like me."

Priscilla leaned forward to Lenny. "You're lucky. I wish I had a little sister instead of a little brother."

"It's not that great," Lenny said softly.

"Yeah," Marigold agreed, but she couldn't help smiling when she thought of how her little sister always called her "Mawigohd." She thought of Lightning, who always kept her company when her parents were busy with Petal. She thought of her parents, who believed in her so much to say that they were sure she would be great at something "rare and wondrous" someday.

WOO! WOO! The whistle interrupted Marigold's thoughts. "Next stop: Winnie's Neighborhood!" the conductor called. "Winnie's Neighborhood, next stop!" Marigold *would* find Winnie and get her magic wand back—she just *had* to if she ever wanted to see her family again.

The train gathered speed more quickly than before. The sound of the engine came fast and furious. *Chugga! Chugga! Chugga!* Faster and faster they barreled along, the noise from the locomotive so loud it made conversation impossible.

WOO! WOO-O-O-O-O-O-O-O-WH! The train ascended into the air. The car tilted to one side, pushing Marigold into Lenny and squishing him against the window. It tilted the other way, and Lenny slid into Marigold, squishing her against the other side of the seat. The train climbed skyward and flew between banks of clouds as tall as skyscrapers. Marigold and Lenny and Priscilla watched spellbound out the window as they swooped past the moon, which seemed close enough to touch. The night sky was bedazzled with stars as bright as jewels.

Marigold watched the landscape change, and after some time, mountains came into view. When the clouds cleared, something caught her eye. It was a tall, lonely mountain with a skinny house several stories high. "It's Winnie's house! It's Winnie's house!" she exclaimed. "Now all we need to do is find Winnie!"

They flew over Spookety Forest, to its farthest corner—an area that Marigold had never been to. Soon the train was spiraling down, down, down. It slowed and came to a halt. The ghost conductor called, "Last stop! All out for Winnie's Neighborhood!"

Marigold stepped outside and peered into the dark, where suspicious eyes gleamed back at her. She had heard that this part of the forest was where the shadow children made their homes, and she knew they'd been taken all the way to Spookety Cave.

12

SPOOKETY CAVE

The ghost train had vanished.

Marigold stood with Lenny and Priscilla on either side of her. The path was nowhere in sight. Marigold shivered and looked to Lenny.

Without her even asking he said, "Eleven fifteen."

Marigold was running out of time.

Priscilla held Boing-Boing tightly. A cold wind blew her black hair wildly about her face. "What's so scary about Super Scary Shadow Boy?"

Lenny spoke in an ominous tone and looked from Marigold to Priscilla. "Super Scary Shadow Boy lives only in darkness."

"Why?" Priscilla asked in a low voice.

"Because he's so hideous to behold!"

Marigold pressed her lips together in consternation. It bothered her that the ghosts, and now even Lenny and Priscilla, couldn't get past the shadow boy's looks. So what if he was only a dark, scary shadow? All he wanted was to have friends.

The ghost children were approaching. Their voices could be heard babbling excitedly.

"I can see you!" said one.

"I can see me!" shouted another.

"We can see one another!" they yelled joyously.

They were visible once more. They flew through the trees, their filmy white gowns glowing in the dark as they tumbled and swung from the branches and swooped through the air, plucking at Marigold's pockets for candy like they always did.

"Thank you, Marigold Star!" they called to her. "Thank you! Thank you! Thank you!" She threw candy up to them, and they caught it and ate it in a flash. But when she told them she wasn't responsible for making them visible, they slowed and swirled about pensively. A ghost girl hovered by Marigold's ear. "Was it . . . the shadow boy?" she hissed.

"Find out, Marigold Star." Another moaned. They all pointed to the dark, gaping hole that formed the mouth of Spookety Cave. "He's in there!"

Marigold squared her shoulders. She had less than forty-five minutes to complete the Invis-O-Friend Spell and get her magic wand back. The only way to do both was to find Winnie and the shadow boy, but Marigold hated caves. They were easy to get lost in, and she'd been warned against them. She took a few steps forward to where it was even darker—at least she had her star to light the way. Still, she hesitated. She didn't want to go any farther alone, but she couldn't ask Lenny and Priscilla to go with her—it was too dangerous. "You stay here," Marigold said. "I'll be back."

Lenny closed his eyes and bowed. "As your trusty sidekick, I am compelled to stick with you till the bitter end," he said solemnly. Then he changed his tone and grinned. "Plus, I wouldn't miss this for anything!" He took Marigold's hand.

Priscilla made a desperate little smile. "Me too," she added, and took Marigold's other hand.

Marigold was surprised but also relieved. She thought

how strange it was that she hadn't known Lenny or Priscilla for very long, but she couldn't think of anyone else, except Lightning, whom she would have wanted with her right now.

Together, all three children entered the cave holding hands.

Marigold's star only partially lit the way, and she had visions of groping through the dark trying to find Winnie in a maze of paths that caves like this were famous for. She worried about getting lost or falling through a hole or being swarmed by bats—or worse.

But they hadn't gone far when Marigold called and a voice called back.

"Winnie?" Marigold shouted. "Are you there?"

"Help, Marigold!" Winnie cried, and she sounded near. "He's made me play Candy Land with him for the last two hours!"

They rounded a corner and entered a rocky chamber. A light twinkled in the dark, just bright enough for Marigold to see that it was coming from her own magic wand. She could see an inky shape with fangs and claws and a long pointy tail—a shape that sat crossed-legged on the magic carpet. Across from him—and with only a board game between them—was unmistakably Winnie.

The girl jumped up and ran to Marigold. She pointed to the shadow boy. "He won't give me back my magic wand!"

Marigold was so happy to see the unpleasant girl that she didn't even have the heart to argue over whose wand it was. "Are you all right, Winnie?"

"I'm fine," she snapped. "It's just that he won't give me my wand and—"

"Marigold Star!" the shadow boy said angrily. "I've been looking for you!" A dark shadow rose and stepped toward Marigold. Lenny and Priscilla recoiled in fear that he might touch them with his scary claws.

He crept closer still. The wand glittered, lighting the dark around him in an enchanted way, and Marigold could see for the first time that he wasn't a shadow but a real creature. "I was supposed to be a superhero—like in your story, Marigold," he said bitterly. He took another step closer. Lenny and Priscilla kept their distance but leaned forward to get a better look, surprised at how much smaller he looked up close than he had as a shadow.

"I thought if I helped the ghosts, they would think I was a

superhero and they would like me. But they didn't. No one likes me." There was a tone of defeat in his voice. "I'm just the same as I've always been—a super-scary-looking monster." He held the wand out, and it trembled in his hands. "Didn't you wonder how the forest appeared everywhere you went in the Human World, Marigold Star?"

Marigold *had* wondered. The forest had first spontaneously appeared in Winnie's neighborhood, then in Lenny's, and finally in Priscilla's. They were all the same Spookety Forest from Bramblycrumbly in three different human places!

"You suddenly vanished. . . . I had to find you, Marigold!" the wretched creature said fiercely. "So I commanded the wand to take me to wherever you were in the Human World."

"But why?" Marigold whispered.

"To give this back." He set the magic wand in her hand. "It's useless to me."

Winnie eyed the wand hungrily. Marigold held it once more, grateful beyond measure. She thanked the shadow boy and extended a hand to him. "Let's be friends."

But he turned his back to her. "You have your wand and

your Winnie and your ghosts. Now leave me alone!"

Marigold was stunned. She slowly withdrew her hand. He'd gone to such great lengths to try to get the ghost children to be friends. It hadn't gone well, and he was discouraged, but what was the alternative? "W-what will you do?" she stammered, for she really couldn't imagine.

He went to his corner, where he was no longer visible. "I will stay here in Spookety Cave by myself and think up make-believe friends to play with." He sighed. "Make-believe friends are so much nicer than real ones!"

No one uttered a word.

Marigold was speechless as well. But there was something about this shadow boy that made her so curious to try to understand him, that even though he clearly didn't want to be friends with her, she couldn't stop herself. She went to him and laid a hand on his shoulder. "There's no need for you to have to imagine a friend to play with because I will always be your friend."

He gazed up at her with distrustful eyes, and Marigold could tell he didn't believe her. Perhaps he thought she was trying to be friends because she felt sorry for him. In any case, her vow of friendship simply wasn't enough. She would have to show him . . . but how? That's when an idea came to Marigold like a thunderbolt. Without a second thought, she reached over her head and took hold of her star. She lifted it from where it had been all her life. It was warm and soft in her hands like sunshine. She tentatively held it over the shadow boy's head, hoping it would stay, and when she took her hands away, it did.

Lenny, Priscilla, and even Winnie gasped.

The shadow boy became completely still, like a startled animal. The star lit him in such a beautiful way that you almost didn't see his teeth or his claws or his sharp tail, and all that was visible were his kind eyes. "Can I keep it . . . forever?" he asked.

Marigold hadn't really thought about *forever.* She glanced upward to where her star had always been. She was used to seeing its glittery light. She was used to feeling its comforting warmth. Having it blink had been upsetting enough. Having it gone was worse than she could have ever imagined.

The shadow boy watched her from beneath the star that sparkled in the most magical way. Of course Marigold had checked to see in mirrors what her star looked like shining over her head, but she'd never seen the star over anybody else's. She had never noticed how it had flecks of silver and gold or the way in which it shimmered that made it look as if it was alive. It was truly stunning and she wanted it back.

The others waited.

Marigold hesitated. She wanted her star back more than anything . . . yet . . . with it shining down on the shadow boy, he wasn't at all as scary as the shadow he projected.

When he looked up at her with his soft brown eyes that had been sad for so long, she just didn't have the heart to take the star away from him. "It's yours to keep," Marigold replied.

All was quiet as the others took this in, until Lenny said in a hushed tone, "This. Is. So. Cool." He rushed up to the shadow boy with such urgency that the creature shrank back in fear. Lenny seemed not to notice. "It's the

confrontation of two opposing forces!" He was bursting with excitement. "Light and dark! Good and evil! Yin and yang!"

Marigold folded her arms. "What *are* you talking about, Lenny?"

"Superheroes, Marigold, superheroes!" he said passionately. "It's inevitable that superheroes who are opposing forces will confront each other—and you two just did!"

"I'm not a superhero, Lenny!" Marigold said for the hundredth time.

"Whatever you say, Marigold." Lenny winked. Then he grinned broadly and stuck out his hand to the shadow boy. "It's an honor to meet you, Mr. Super Scary Shadow Boy."

The creature shook his head. "I'm not a superhero either."

Lenny's eyes bugged out. "Are you kidding me?" He took hold of the shadow boy's paw and pumped it furiously. "You are an incredible, awesome superhero!"

"I am?" the shadow boy said in a small voice.

Priscilla came forward too. "A pleasure to meet you, Mr. Shadow Boy." She shook his paw as well. "Lenny has told me so much about you."

"He has?" the creature asked, bewildered.

"Oh yes!" Priscilla exclaimed. "He showed me your comic book."

Lenny whipped the comic out of his back pocket. "Oh my gosh! Could you sign this for me?" He felt around in all his pockets and produced a pen.

"But . . . but . . . where did this come from?" the shadow boy asked.

Winnie looked over his shoulder at it. "You mean he really is a superhero?"

Lenny pointed to a page. "Could you write, 'To Lenny, an awesome comic book fan if there ever was one,' or whatever you want is okay or just— No, wait. 'To Lenny . . . my awesome friend.' Could you underline 'friend'?"

While the shadow boy wrote the inscription, Winnie whispered in Marigold's ear, "Who is that kid?"

"That's Lenny," Marigold replied.

"He's the biggest weirdo I've ever seen," Winnie said. "And who's the other kid with the cat?"

"That's Priscilla. She's very nice," Marigold said.

"I don't like her—she's got bangs." Winnie sniffed.

"But you've got bangs," Marigold said.

"I know, but her bangs are creepy." Winnie stamped her foot. "Are you really not going to let me carry that magic wand?"

Marigold gave her a look that said she really was not going to let the girl carry her wand.

Lenny blew on the page for the ink to dry. "There's just one more thing. . . ." He hesitated. "I don't want to overstep or anything but . . ."

Everybody waited.

"You know what would be super awesome and like *so* cool?" Lenny straightened his glasses. When no one asked "What?" he continued. "You know how Marigold gave you her a-*maz*-ing star? If you could give Marigold something equally a-*maz*-ing . . ."

"Like what?" the shadow boy asked.

"Um, how about your Candy Land game?" Lenny said. "It would just make it *so* perfect!"

"Lenny!" Marigold scolded.

"Too much? Sorry, it's just that you gave him something awesome, and it would be so cool if he gave you something awesome in return—like an exchange of superhero awesomeness."

"I'm not a superhero," Marigold said wearily.

"Lenny is right." The shadow boy handed her the game.

"But you love Candy Land." Marigold didn't want to take his favorite game, but the creature shook his shaggy head and insisted she have it.

Lenny was already running outside and calling to the ghosts. "Guys! Guys!" The ghosts gathered and were agog over all the pictures Lenny showed them of themselves in the pages of his comic book. The shadow boy appeared from the cave, and the ghost children were even more surprised and dazzled by the golden sparkly starlight over his head. They admired it and forgot that they were ever scared of him.

"He's not even a shadow! He really *is* a superhero!" they said, and then argued over who knew this to be true all along.

"I was never really afraid of him," one ghost child bragged.

"Me either," another was quick to add.

"Yes, you were," his sister said.

"I was not!" he yelled.

"You were too!" she yelled back.

They squabbled back and forth and swirled through the trees.

WOO! WOO! The train whistle sounded, and in seconds, it rolled into view.

The ghost children flew to it, and the shadow boy scrambled onto the train platform, the star over his head glowing brighter than ever.

"You were right, Marigold Star!" the ghost children called to her. "Super Scary Shadow Boy is an incredible superhero!"

"And so is Marigold Star!" the shadow boy shouted joyfully.

Marigold watched with despair as the ghost train swirled into the sky and flew over the tops of the trees, then vanished in the mist along with her star. She didn't care what anyone said: she wasn't a superhero—and she couldn't help thinking that she had just made another super mistake.

13

BROWNIES!

Marigold stood gazing off into the distance with thoughts of home filling her mind. She wondered what everyone would say. She wondered if they would still call her Marigold Star . . . or if they would call her Marigold Starless? One thing was for sure: they wouldn't say she was marked for greatness anymore.

While Marigold mulled this over, Winnie took advantage of the moment. "I'll take that!" she said, and snatched the wand right out of Marigold's hand.

"Hey!" Marigold shouted. "Give it back!"

"No way," Winnie replied.

Marigold couldn't believe she'd not only given away her star but now she'd lost her magic wand for the third time that night. *I am truly hopeless*, Marigold thought, then she pleaded with the girl to give it back. She couldn't tell Winnie that she needed to make friends with her—that was against the rules of the spell (which carried dire consequences, like having to spend the rest of her life in the Human World)—but she tried to tell Winnie that without her wand, something terrible might happen in Bramblycrumbly. Marigold glanced at Lenny.

"Eleven forty," he answered.

"Hmmm . . ." Winnie stroked her chin. She spoke as if she was thinking out loud. "If something terrible happens in Bramblycrumbly you might not be able to go back . . . and you'd have to stay here."

A cold wind whistled through the trees. It was just too awful a thought for Marigold to consider. All the petals on her head drooped, her pink tights were ripped, and her sky-blue dress was far too thin for this world.

"You're shivering," Winnie said sternly. She swung the green cape with the big gold star over Marigold's shoulders. "The last thing I need is for you to catch cold."

Lenny and Priscilla looked on in awkward silence. Marigold was glad to have the cape and pulled it around herself to keep out the cold, but what she really wanted from Winnie was her magic wand! She weighed the odds of whether she might be able to snatch it away from the girl, when without warning, a loud thrashing sound came from the brush. Right in front of them, Meatball raced by with Winnie's bag of candy clenched tightly between his teeth. Norman was right behind him.

Winnie's eyes almost popped out of her head. "My candy!" Expertly, she wished on the magic wand to make the dog stop. He came to a screeching halt and dropped the bag at Winnie's feet. "Good dog," she purred. But when she looked, a hole had been gnawed in the bottom of it. The bag was empty. "You ate all my candy!" she said in disbelief. Winnie took the magic wand and smacked the dog on his snout.

"Hey!" Norman cried. "You can't do that!"

"Gr-r-r-r," said Meatball. He grabbed the end of the wand in his teeth.

"Give it back." Winnie struggled with dog over the wand, and they were soon in a tug-of-war. Meatball gave it one last mighty tug. He stood still for a second, the wand firmly in his mouth. Winnie's face was a mixture of surprise and horror. Then the dog whirled around and took off into the forest.

The magic carpet safely rolled up under her arm—for without the magic wand, Winnie wasn't taking any chances of having that snatched away from her too—she took off in hot pursuit, with Norman right on her heels. "Come back here, Meatball!" they both screamed.

Marigold, Lenny, and Priscilla—with Boing-Boing held tightly in her arms—ran to catch up. They chased after Winnie and Norman out of the forest, past a ball field, through a neighborhood, and by a school. They finally found Winnie and Norman behind the community center, but Meatball was gone.

"We lost him!" Winnie said angrily.

But as they all stood catching their breaths, they heard the sound of barking.

"I'd know that bark anywhere." Norman pointed to a huge tent. "It's Meatball!"

Marigold watched Winnie stride up to the tent and yank away the flap. "Brownies!" Winnie yelled.

"Seepage," Marigold gasped. She could feel her legs go weak at the thought of a whole tent full of brownies in

control of her magic wand. But how had brownies seeped into the Human World? Winnie hadn't wished for them. Had the shadow boy somehow done it while he was in possession of her wand? Her mind reeled. There was no way she could ever get the wand away from a bunch of brownies. Priscilla grabbed her by the sleeve. "I can't look," Marigold muttered.

"It's just Brownies." Priscilla pulled Marigold inside the tent. "I'm Priscilla, and this is my friend Marigold."

"Where?" the Brownies asked.

"Here," Priscilla replied.

Marigold peeked through her fingers to see several girls wearing brown beanies and sashes full of merit badges. Some held bags of marshmallows, others graham crackers and chocolate bars. She had never been so relieved to see not one real brownie in sight. "Um, Priscilla, they can't see me. Lenny thinks it's because he made me up—but it really has something to do with the spell I said to find you."

"Here!" Priscilla held up her cat. The Brownies gazed at Priscilla with blank faces. "I mean, this is my friend *Boing-Boing*—my *other* cat is *Marigold*." Priscilla made an embarrassed little laugh, and the Brownies giggled. Sitting in the middle of them was Meatball, barking for them to feed him the marshmallows that were for their s'mores. Winnie stood awkwardly in the center of the tent holding the magic wand once more.

"Say hello to the girls," Marigold instructed.

"Hi, everyone. I'm Winnie." She held out her hand.

"But aren't you the girl who doesn't like anybody?" the Brownies asked.

"Yes," Winnie replied.

"Say no," Marigold quickly whispered in her ear.

"I mean, no." Winnie shook their hands.

"Quick, ask them if they want to be friends," Marigold said.

Winnie tilted her head. "Why?"

Marigold thought that maybe the first step toward making friends with Winnie was to show her how. "Just ask them, Winnie," Marigold said softly. "You'll see why."

Winnie wrinkled her nose, but she did as Marigold instructed. "Want to be friends?" she asked tentatively.

"Introduce Norman and Lenny and Priscilla," Marigold suggested.

"This is Norman and his dog, Meatball," Winnie said.

But when she went to introduce Lenny, he was nowhere to be found.

Marigold went outside to look for the shy boy and found him hiding behind some garbage cans.

"Come and meet the Brownies, Lenny," Marigold said.

"That's okay," Lenny replied. "I'm good."

"Come on, Lenny," Marigold said.

He folded his arms and stuck out his chin stubbornly. "I told you, I'm afraid of people, and that includes Brownies."

Marigold tried to entice him with s'mores, and when he wouldn't budge even a smidge, she took hold of his hands and pulled him to a standing position. "You didn't like Priscilla when you first met her either," she reminded him.

"But she likes comic books," Lenny mumbled.

Marigold was losing patience. "You can't be friends only with people who like comic books!"

Lenny shrugged. "Why not?"

"Because you're missing out on a lot of fun, Lenny!" she shouted out of frustration.

Lenny studied her with a steady gaze. "So are you, Marigold."

Marigold pointed at herself. "Me?" She had no idea what he was talking about.

"By not flying!" Lenny cried. "This is the part of the story where you should have overcome your temporary lapse of confidence and realized that you can fly!"

"But I can't fly!" Marigold stamped her foot and shouted at the boy, "I'm afraid!"

"I told you, it's just your timing that's off, Marigold. Just leap as you say the word 'fly.' Don't be afraid!"

Marigold tried once more. She swung her arms on the word "magic," but she leaped before she said "poket." "Fly!" she exclaimed, and landed—*thud*—in the dirt. "See?" Marigold angrily brushed leaves and dirt off her dress. "I can't fly!"

"Yes, you *can*," Lenny said fiercely. "You have to leap on the word 'fly.' You're so close to getting it, Marigold! Try once more! Don't be afraid!"

Marigold had had enough. "When are you going to understand that I'm not one of your stupid superheroes!"

Lenny stood motionless, and his eyes filled with tears.

Marigold tossed her head. "I'm not a superhero!"

"Okay, fine," Lenny said. He turned and walked away from her. "You're not a superhero."

Marigold called after him, "And you're just a boy who reads a lot of comic books—it doesn't make you an expert!"

Lenny kept walking. Marigold watched him go straight to the tent. He shoved away the flap, and Marigold got there in time to see him shaking with fear as he said, "H-Hi, I—I'm Lenny." He turned and looked longingly at the exit of the tent, and for a moment Marigold thought he was going to flee. Instead, he took a deep breath. "Um, like, what are all your n-names or whatever?" he asked.

One by one, the girls told Lenny their names. Then someone asked him if he wanted a s'more. He stood there clumsily, trying to eat it, and chocolate dribbled down the front of his hoodie. Priscilla patted the space next to her. "Sit here, Lenny," she said.

He sat, and this time when he ate his s'more, it didn't dribble. Soon he was laughing with the others at Boing-Boing, who, as it turned out, liked marshmallows too.

The Brownies showed Winnie, Lenny, and Priscilla how to make s'mores. Then they all sat around eating them till there were no more left.

Marigold whispered in Winnie's ear, "Invite everyone to your birthday party."

Winnie did, adding, "And bring Meatball!"

Marigold noticed that the girl's cheeks were flushed and

her eyes sparkled. Winnie actually looked happy for a change. Marigold was happy because Winnie was happy— they had shared "joy"—she checked it off the list from the Invis-O-Friend Spell. Now all Marigold had to do was to get Winnie to share laughter, sorrow, and advice with her.

It was very late by now. Norman waved goodbye, saying he'd see Winnie the next day, and took Meatball home.

The Brownies were tired and said goodbye, agreeing to meet the next day at Winnie's house as well. "Don't wake up our moms!" a Brownie said, and giggled.

Outside, Winnie, Lenny, and Priscilla and Boing-Boing tiptoed past another tent they assumed was where some of the Brownies' mothers were staying.

As soon as they were far enough away not to be seen or heard, Winnie said she could take Priscilla and Lenny home. Everyone was in high spirits at the prospect of a ride on a flying carpet . . . everyone except Marigold, who was too worried. It had to be after midnight by now. It gave her a tight feeling in her stomach, and all she could do was hope that Winnie's birthday was on this day but hours from now.

As they seated themselves on the carpet, Marigold

glanced at Lenny to see if she could get his attention. He always had a way of making her feel better, and maybe he had some great comic book advice on how there was no way that Bramblycrumbly had just crumbled. She tried to catch his eye, but he turned away. She stared at the side of his head, but he wouldn't look at her. Marigold whispered, "See? I told you it was easy to make friends." But he wouldn't answer her. He acted like she was invisible.

This gave Marigold a disturbing thought. Maybe Lenny could no longer see her because he had made friends of his own. Maybe she had unwittingly completed the Invis-O-Friend Spell that had brought her to him. Maybe she had missed another page of the spell book where this rule was written. "Lenny! Can't you see me anymore? Say something—please!"

To Marigold's surprise, Lenny turned to her and said calmly, "Actually, I'm not speaking to you right now because I don't speak to people who call superheroes *stupid* . . . but . . . if I were speaking to you—which I'm not—I'd say that making friends just now was about as easy for me as flying is for you." Then he turned his head and wouldn't say another word.

Marigold was alternately relieved and uneasy. She'd never had a friend not speak to her—it was unnerving.

Winnie held the magic wand tightly in her fist, and it glittered like it never had before. The carpet rippled enticingly as it hovered a few inches off the ground. A chill wind blew, and Marigold watched, impressed with Winnie's magic wand skills as the girl delivered a command. "Magic wand . . . give us a soft, warm, blue blanket with gold stars on it. Make it big enough for four kids and a large cat!"

BANGO! FLUFF!

A soft, warm, midnight-blue blanket with gold stars appeared, covering them all and neatly tucking itself around them. Then Winnie commanded, "Magic flying carpet . . . take me, Marigold, Priscilla and Boing-Boing, and Lenny to Lenny's home and then Priscilla's—and make it snappy!"

ZIZZLE! MUSH!

The carpet rose in the air and circled over the community center, over the Brownies' tent, and away past Spookety Forest into the starry night. From under the blanket, the little group watched, cozy and warm, as the flying carpet weaved them expertly in and out of tall banks of clouds.

Below, the lights from towns twinkled. They soared across a breathtaking sky, all awestruck except for Priscilla, who hardly noticed. She cradled the large orange cat in her arms and looked deeply into his eyes as if she was trying to memorize every whisker on his face.

With a melancholy meow, Boing-Boing squirmed in her arms and reached up to lick her nose. As wondrous and dizzying as the flying carpet ride was on such a glorious night, it was still hard not to feel sad for the girl.

"Don't worry, Priscilla, I'll take Boing-Boing," Lenny said gently. Priscilla let him hold the cat, who stared balefully up at the boy. "I love cats!" Lenny said brightly. "ACHOO! ACHOO! AH-AH-AH-AH-CHOO! It's just that . . . ACHOO! I'm allergic to him." He handed Boing-Boing back.

Everyone now was sorry for Priscilla, especially Marigold, who wished she could help her friend. "Give Boing-Boing to me."

"Really?" Priscilla said, surprised. "You're not allergic to him?"

"Not at all." Marigold had always wanted a cat, and she knew that Lightning would love Boing-Boing as much as she did.

The cat purred in Marigold's arms, and Priscilla looked much relieved. But there was still something that worried Marigold about Priscilla, because she had not been successful in finding the girl a nice little cottage in the woods. "Are you sure you want to return home, Priscilla? You won't be too lonely?"

Just then they flew over the park with the picnic area where they'd found Priscilla. She shook her head. "When my old next-door neighbor moved, I thought I would never find another friend as good as her. I had hopes when a new family moved in because there was a boy my own age."

The carpet curved around a chimney.

"There's my house!" Lenny shouted. They settled in the front yard, and Lenny sprang off the carpet.

So did Priscilla. She stood before Lenny grinning. "But the new boy never came outside."

"You live here?" Lenny pointed to the house next to his with disbelief.

"Mm-hm. See you tomorrow?" Priscilla said a little shyly.

"See you tomorrow," Lenny replied.

The door to Priscilla's house opened. "Priscilla!" someone shouted, and the girl ran to them. Marigold watched

Priscilla hug her mom and dad and her little brother, and her heart ached for her own family—even her little sister, Petal.

"Goodbye!" Winnie called to Priscilla and Lenny.

"Goodbye!" Marigold called as well. Priscilla waved.

"Lenny?" Marigold said hesitantly.

"If I was speaking to you, Marigold, I'd say goodbye right now, but since I'm not speaking to you, I won't say goodbye." Lenny turned and made his way to the front door of his house. Marigold felt so bad about what she had said and wished she could take it all back. She was so impressed by how brave he had been, walking into the tent full of girls he didn't know—she knew how much courage it must have taken. . . . Probably more courage than it would take for her to stop being afraid to fly.

"Magic flying carpet, take Marigold and me home!" Winnie commanded. Right away, the carpet zoomed upward into the sky. It swooped in a long arc back in the direction from where they'd just come, but Marigold had never felt worse. She had hurt Lenny's feelings. She watched the back of the boy making his way up the walk, his figure growing smaller and smaller the farther away they flew. Lenny's words echoed in her ears: "Just leap when you say the word 'fly.' Don't be afraid!"

He was almost at his door. He'd been such a good friend. He'd had so much belief in her—more than she'd had in herself. She couldn't let him go—not like this. She just had to say she was sorry.

"Spoket! Spoket! Magic poket! Fly!" Marigold leaped into the air with all her might, flying off the magic carpet just at the right moment to get back to Lenny. She was flying! "Lenny!" Marigold yelled as loudly as she could. In what seemed like seconds, she was at his side and speaking breathlessly. "I'm sorry, Lenny—I never meant to hurt your feelings. . . . Do you forgive me?"

"You flew," Lenny whispered.

"I didn't mean what I said about superheroes being stupid," Marigold said earnestly.

Lenny's eyes lit up. "You didn't?"

"No!" Marigold exclaimed. "I was just frustrated that I couldn't fly—and you kept telling me I could and—"

"Oh. My. Gosh." Lenny stared at Marigold.

"W-what?" Marigold stammered. "Is something wrong?"

"We're having a peak experience of higher consciousness," Lenny said with growing wonder.

Marigold had no idea what he was talking about.

"Okay, okay." Lenny raised his eyes and held his hands out palms down, as if he had to stop everything in order to explain this important point. "Look, you said that superheroes were stupid, right?"

"And I'm totally sorry now, Lenny—"

Lenny waved her apology aside. "Now I see that you only said that because of your fear of not measuring up to the standard of superhero awesomeness because of your inability to fly. Now that you can fly, you see I was right: superheroes aren't stupid." Lenny stopped to see if Marigold was following his train of thought.

She wasn't.

He continued. "Alternately, *I* see that you really didn't mean what *you* said, but hearing you call superheroes stupid made me so angry that it pushed *me* to march into that tent full of Brownies, thus overcoming *my* fear of people." Lenny ran a hand shaking with excitement over his forehead. "It's a *catharsis*!" He stood gazing at her with admiration and joy. "For both of us!"

"For both of us!" Marigold exclaimed, still not sure what a catharsis was but just happy that they were back to being friends again.

Winnie zoomed up to Marigold with her flying carpet.

"And one more thing." Lenny held out his watch to show Marigold the time. "Don't worry that it's after midnight. . . . It's this thing about being a superhero? Just when you think all is lost . . . it isn't. There's always the all-important secret twist at the end that you'd never expect."

Marigold scrunched up her nose. "The secret twist?"

"Yeah—you'll see. The important thing for a superhero to remember is to never lose faith." Lenny saluted Marigold.

It might have been the cape, but she wondered if the comic book–loving boy had been right after all, because for the first time she felt like a real superhero. Then again, with a friend like Lenny, how could she not?

She waved goodbye to Lenny, and he waved back. Then she turned to Winnie, who sat with Boing-Boing on the flying carpet. It seemed to vibrate with energy.

"Get on," Winnie ordered.

Marigold had to laugh. "You know, Winnie, you really ought to try to be less bossy."

Winnie laughed too. "Okay, but don't think you're getting your magic wand. I know you'll go right back to Brambly-crumbly, and I'm having way too much fun with you right here!" With that, Winnie commanded the magic carpet to take them home.

Marigold's smile faded as she checked "laughter" off the list now too. Clearly it was going to be a struggle to get her magic wand back. A tingle of dread slithered up Marigold's spine to think of what would happen if she didn't.

14

ADVICE AND SORROW

Zooooom! Fizzz!

They shot up into the sky.

Boing-Boing snuggled between Marigold and Winnie under the warm blanket. They flew through the night and watched the moon go down. By the time the tall, lonely mountain came into view, it was morning. As the first rays of light appeared over the horizon, Marigold braced herself for the task ahead, and hoped with all her heart that Winnie had not yet officially turned nine years old. The carpet circled Winnie's house and flew in through the same window that was still open from the evening before.

No sooner were they back in Winnie's bedroom than her mother appeared at the door. "Happy Birthday, Winnie Binnie!"

"Quick, Winnie!" Marigold pleaded. "Ask her what time you'll turn nine today."

Winnie made a face. "What's so important about having to know what time I'll turn nine today?"

"Oh, it's very important!" her mom exclaimed. "I remember the day and time you were born like it was yesterday!" She smiled to herself. "I'll never forget because the doctor said, 'Good, I have fourteen minutes to get to my Zumba class at seven thirty! So, you were born exactly at seven sixteen at night."

"Seven sixteen?" Marigold did a cartwheel. "There's still time!"

Winnie stood with her hands on her hips. "Are you sure you didn't just see that?"

"See what, sweetums?" her mother asked.

Winnie exhaled loudly. "A girl? With flowers for hair? Just did a cartwheel right under your nose?"

"You are a silly girl." Her mother turned to leave. "Seven sixteen, nine years ago," she said. "Feels like it was yesterday."

Marigold was beside herself with joy. She still had time to complete the spell, get her magic wand back, and save

Bramblycrumbly. "Advice" and "sorrow"—those were all she had to share with Winnie and the spell would be complete!

Winnie watched Marigold suspiciously. "What's wrong with you?"

"I'm just happy!" Marigold did another cartwheel.

Winnie tilted her head and narrowed her eyes. "Why?"

"Um, because it's your birthday today," Marigold replied. She didn't dare tell Winnie the real reason—the small print from the Invis-O-Friend Spell had warned her not to.

The entire morning, Marigold followed Winnie around and tried her best to get the girl to give her some advice. She asked Winnie about the weather. Did she think it might rain? Did she think it called for a raincoat or an umbrella? Boots or galoshes?

"How should I know?" Winnie answered.

Marigold persisted. Did she know a good cure for hiccups? Or where to buy a toothbrush? Oven mitts? Gumdrops? Winnie just shrugged. Marigold tried harder. What were easier to make: muffins or pies? How would Winnie spell the word "argyle"? Or fold a sweater? Underwear? A bathing suit? To which side of the plate would a glass go when setting a table?

"You're driving me crazy!" Winnie shouted. "Stop asking me all these questions!"

But Marigold couldn't stop—Bramblycrumbly depended on her getting advice from Winnie! How do you make a square knot? she asked. Sew on a button? Throw out a garbage can? But no matter what Marigold asked Winnie, she would not offer any advice.

This was going to be a lot harder than Marigold had previously thought.

All morning it seemed like someone from Winnie's family called to say, "Happy Birthday." First it was her grandmother, then an aunt. Two cousins called and an uncle. Marigold didn't know if she was just tired—after all, she'd been awake all night—but by afternoon, even though she knew she should be happy to see Winnie enjoying the attention and being friendly (for she had improved much in that department), Marigold couldn't stop worrying.

"Aren't you exhausted?" Winnie asked. She lay down on her bed, tucked the magic wand under her pillow, and added, "Just so you know—I'm a light sleeper."

Marigold was far too worried to sleep. Instead, she sat on

Winnie's bed, petting Boing-Boing and wondering if she'd ever be able to complete the Invis-O-Friend Spell in time. The longer she sat thinking, the more upset she became.

When Winnie woke up, Marigold was on the verge of tears. "Okay, so what's the matter with you *now*?" Winnie asked.

Marigold appealed to Winnie one more time for her magic wand.

"Nonsense," Winnie replied. "What you really need is a star!" She took the magic wand out from under the pillow and said, "Magic wand ... put a gold star over Marigold's head."

TWINK!

But the star that appeared over Marigold's head was all wrong. It was too small. It was dull.

Winnie tried again. "Magic wand ... get rid of the star that's over Marigold's head and replace it with a bigger, brighter star!"

TWINKY! ZAP!

Even Boing-Boing was startled, and he ran to hide under the bed because this time the star was neon pink and not the right shape.

On the third try, the star was lopsided.

The fourth was much too big.

The fifth had green and yellow sparkles around it and didn't look a thing like her old star.

No matter how detailed Winnie gave orders to the magic wand, the star turned out just not to be the same.

"Forget it," Winnie finally said. It was one o'clock and almost time for her party.

Marigold took Boing-Boing out from under the bed. "All my friends in Bramblycrumbly will just have to call me Marigold Starless from now on."

"Don't worry about that," Winnie replied. "You're not going back to Bramblycrumbly—you're staying right here to be *my* friend!" With the wand clenched in her tight little fist, she turned on her heel and hurried off to get dressed for her birthday party.

That afternoon, Winnie's party was a rousing success. The Brownies came, and Norman and Meatball too. Marigold still hadn't been able to get Winnie to give her advice—but Marigold continued to offer advice to Winnie, hoping that if Winnie had some friends, she wouldn't mind it so much if Marigold went home.

190

"Say thank you," Marigold said during the present-opening ceremony when Winnie unwrapped a plastic water bottle with the name of the local gas station on it.

"But it's not even a real present," Winnie whispered.

"It's the thought that counts," Marigold said. "Say thank you anyway."

And Winnie did.

During the games, Marigold told Winnie to let someone else win.

"Why?" Winnie asked.

"Because it will be more fun for your guests," Marigold said.

Winnie let two of the Brownies win, and she made sure everyone had enough cake because Marigold told her to check on that as well. Marigold was sure no one would ever call Winnie the most unfriendly girl in town ever again.

After the games, the cake, and all the presents, after everyone had gone home, Winnie said, "I never knew how much fun having friends could be!"

"See?" Marigold said.

"You were right," Winnie said. "But you were wrong about something."

They were sitting with the big orange cat under the black glittery chandelier on Winnie's bed. Winnie held the wand, and it twinkled and shimmered spectacularly. With a flip of the wrist, she wrote her name in the air with glittery stars. "There's absolutely nothing wrong with this magic wand," Winnie said with glee.

Marigold had to admit that Winnie was right. "How do you make it work so well?"

"You have to be clear, Marigold. You have to say exactly what you want. Remember that!" Winnie instructed.

"Thank you!" Marigold said. Not only had Winnie finally offered her some advice, it was actually very good advice. She finally was able to check it off the list because now they'd both shared some with each other.

Winnie noticed. "Why do you keep checking things off that list?"

"Because when everything is checked, the spell is complete. . . ." Marigold glanced anxiously at the clock on the nightstand. She still had an hour to share "sorrow."

"And when the spell is complete, then what? Will you leave?" Winnie asked softly.

Marigold nodded. "But—I can't without my wand."

"Good! You'll stay forever." Winnie shoved the wand out of sight under her pillow.

Just then Winnie's mother appeared at the door. "Oh, honey, I wanted to tell you I was a bit mistaken earlier. I remember it now so clearly. It wasn't a doctor, it was a *nurse* who said, 'Good! Now I can make my *pilates*'—not Zumba—'class at six thirty!" So, it wasn't seven sixteen when you were born, bunny rabbit. . . . It was actually six sixteen." Her mother disappeared from the doorway. "You're officially nine years old, Winnie Binnie!" she sang out.

"NO-O-O!" Marigold groaned, and fell facedown on the bed. Winnie couldn't have already turned nine. Marigold hadn't completed the spell yet and she didn't have her magic wand back—which meant . . . at this very moment, Brambycrumbly was crumbling and turning to brambles! What had happened to her friends? Her family? Her dragon? She burst into tears.

Winnie stared at her in bewilderment. "Why are you crying?"

Marigold got up on one elbow and took big gulping breaths. She could barely speak. "B-Bramblyc-c-crumbly has crumbled! A-and it's all my f-f-f-f-fault!"

"What are you talking about?" Winnie said.

Marigold was too upset to explain. She scooped up Boing-Boing and climbed off the bed. "I have to leave right away, Winnie—*please* give me back my magic wand! I need to figure out what to do. Bramblycrumbly has crumbled. It's nothing but b-b-b-b-b-brambles!" She hiccupped.

"How do you know?" Winnie asked. "Maybe you're wrong."

Marigold shook her head vehemently. "The spell book said so."

"But maybe it's wrong. . . . Maybe all is not lost," Winnie said.

Marigold almost dropped Boing-Boing. She stopped crying and placed the cat back on the bed. "What did you just say?" she whispered.

Winnie's mouth opened, and her eyes went wide as she tried to think of what she'd just said. "Um . . . the spell book? All is not lost?"

"The spell book—the lost pages!" Marigold wiped her cheeks with the back of her hand as she remembered Lenny's parting words: *Just when you think all is lost . . . it isn't. There's always the all-important secret twist at the end that you'd never expect.* Maybe the lost pages in the spell book were the secret twist that Lenny was talking about! "Oh, Winnie, please give me back my wand."

Now it was Winnie's turn to cry. Her lower lip trembled. "If you go . . . can you come back?"

Marigold wasn't sure. "I—I don't know," she said. She could feel fresh tears spring to her eyes because she had come to really like Winnie and couldn't stand to think of never seeing her again.

Now they both cried, and Marigold would have checked "sorrow" off the list except it didn't matter anymore. She and Winnie were officially friends, but it was too late.

Winnie blew her nose and handed Marigold a tissue. "Even if you never come back . . . can we stay friends forever and ever anyway?" She took the wand from under her pillow and clutched it to her chest.

"Forever and ever," Marigold promised. She took off the green cape with the big gold star that she was still wearing and gave it back to Winnie.

Winnie gave the wand back to Marigold. It had never sparkled so brightly. "Tell it to take you home, Marigold. . . .

Remember to be clear!"

"I will." Marigold took the wand with much trepidation, not knowing what to expect. She thanked Winnie from the bottom of her heart. Marigold marveled that Winnie seemed like an entirely different girl than the one whose room she had found herself in the night before—and what a good friend she had turned out to be. She squeezed the girl's hand and said, "Remember to be friendly, Winnie."

"I will," Winnie promised.

Marigold gathered Boing-Boing and her Candy Land game in her arms. She took a deep breath and said, "Magic wand . . . take me home!"

"Goodbye, Marigold!" Winnie called.

Marigold called back, "Goodbye, Winnie!"

SHOOSH! POP! POOF!

15

MAGIC POWERS

"Who's Winnie?" a voice said.

"Lightning!" Marigold ran to her dragon. She threw her arms around his neck and squeezed him tight.

"Whoa!" He laughed. "What's that for?"

"Are you okay?" She released the dragon and held him at arm's length to give him a good once-over. Satisfied that he looked exactly the same, she hugged him again as if she would never let him go.

"I'm fine, but—" Lightning stared at Boing-Boing, who stood in the middle of Marigold's bedroom eyeing the dragon's bed with the comfy down pillow by the fire. "Who's that?" Lightning asked.

"That's Priscilla's cat, Boing-Boing," Marigold answered.

"Who's Priscilla?" The dragon looked confused.

Marigold was in too much of a hurry to answer. She bolted to the window and was relieved to see that outside, Bramblycrumbly appeared to be exactly the same too. "Oh, Lightning, I'll tell you everything later!" she exclaimed. "But I've been on the most incredible adventure—did you miss me?"

"Miss you?" He sounded truly puzzled. "You haven't even been gone five minutes!"

Now Marigold was the one to be confused. She knew she'd been gone an entire day!

Lightning continued. "You said the Invis-O-Friend Spell, and then you disappeared like *that*." He snapped his fingers. "And now you're back."

Marigold didn't understand. *How could five minutes in Bramblycrumbly be the same as twenty-four hours in the Human World? Unless . . .* Little waves of incredulity washed over her. "Unless . . . maybe this is the secret twist—just like Lenny predicted," she whispered to herself.

Lightning didn't seem to have heard. "Where's your star?" He wore a worried look.

"Not now, Lightning!" Marigold grabbed his hand to pull

him over to the window. "We have to go right away to talk to Granny Cabbage."

Lightning resisted and looked back at the big orange cat who was awkwardly climbing into his bed. "But—But what about learning the Invisibility Spell?"

Marigold took out her magic wand.

"You found it!" the dragon exclaimed.

"Watch this." Marigold took her right foot off the ground. She rubbed her stomach, tapped her head, crossed her eyes, and said, "Magic wand . . . make me invisible!"

POOF! She disappeared.

"WOW!" said Lightning.

A moment later she materialized and scooped up Boing-Boing. She flung open the window and stood on the ledge.

"Be careful!" Lightning rushed to her side just as she said the spell, leaped into the air, and shouted, "FLY!"

He poked his head out the window. "Since when do you fly?"

"Follow me!" Marigold called back. "And bring the Candy Land game!"

"B-but it has a picture of *humans* on it, and—" Lightning stammered.

"Bring it anyway!" Marigold shouted, and flew away into the dark night. She passed over Mrs. Moon's tree, Bob the Woodcutter's Son's stacks of wood, and Baddie Longlegs's shack under the bridge. She flew as fast as she could over Spookety Forest, not pausing until she came to the old cabbage lady's little cottage on the other side of the woods. Before Marigold could knock on the door, it opened. There stood Granny Cabbage. "I've been expecting you, child." She motioned them inside.

Lightning pointed to the blank space above Marigold's head. "Her star is missing, Granny!"

"I can see that," she said with less concern than Marigold thought she should have had.

Marigold hurried indoors. Lightning followed behind, so flustered that he knocked a bunch of dried oregano off one of the rafters. He turned to pick it up and his tail caught several garden shears, which clattered noisily to the floor. Granny seemed to take no notice.

It seemed like ages ago since Marigold had sat in the same chair by the fire with her feet tucked under her, but now she had Boing-Boing on her lap. Lightning once again plunked himself down on the cushion. Marigold hardly knew where to begin. "Oh, Granny! Bramblycrumbly almost crumbled! And I lost my wand—even though you warned me not to—and I gave my star away! What will my parents say? What will everyone think?"

The wise old cabbage sat in her stuffed chair like before, with her feet up on the burlap bag of wood chips. "Tell me everything. Start at the beginning."

Marigold took a deep breath to calm down. Then she told Granny how it all began with the Invisibility Spell and how it had actually worked—but on her wand, which had vanished.

Granny raised an eyebrow but said nothing.

"The spell book said that it was easier to find an invisible magic wand if *I* was invisible. Right away, I found the Invis-O-Friend Spell that I could perform without a magic wand." Marigold leaned forward earnestly. "Granny . . . the next thing I knew I was in the *Human* World, where I met a human girl named Winnie, and *she* had my magic wand."

The old cabbage lady betrayed little emotion, like a stern judge listening to someone on the witness stand.

"Winnie wouldn't give it back, and then something *really* bad happened. . . ." Marigold looked around before she even uttered the awful word. "Seepage," she hissed.

Granny closed her eyes and nodded solemnly.

Marigold pressed on. "Winnie wished for ghosts, and with them was a shadow boy. He snatched the wand away from Winnie to make the ghost children visible so they would like him, but as soon as they saw his scary shadow they were afraid and flew away."

Granny rested her elbows on the arms of the chair, and her fingers touched to form a little steeple. She listened intently. Lightning, on the other hand, was full of questions. "Did you chase after them?" he asked.

"Yes!" Marigold told him how Winnie had ordered a magic carpet earlier while she had the wand and that they'd flown on that, but it hadn't been long before she'd lost Winnie because her star began to blink.

"Again?" Lightning said with disbelief.

"I said the Invis-O-Friend Spell, thinking it would take me to Winnie, but I ended up in the bedroom of a boy named Lenny!" Marigold explained her entire adventure— about Spookety Forest appearing everywhere she went, meeting Priscilla, and finally ending up in Spookety Cave. As she spoke, Marigold knew her story sounded altogether absurd, as if she'd dreamed it or made it up. She was glad for the Candy Land game because wouldn't that at least be some evidence that she'd really been in the Human World?

"But how did you lose your star?" Lightning wanted to know.

Marigold glanced at Granny, who sat quietly observing her.

"I gave my star to the shadow boy—but he's not a shadow at all, Granny. He's a terribly nice little creature. My star lights him up so that the ghost children can see he's not scary, and now they're all friends." Marigold tilted her head. "Do you believe me? Because if you don't, I brought that." She nodded to where Lightning had set the Candy Land game as far away from himself as he could, on top of a barrel of chestnuts. "It's a game from the Human World called Candy Land."

Granny's face crinkled with astonishment. "My word!" She heaved herself out of the chair and crossed the room to get a better look. "I've been trying to find that for years— wherever did you get it?"

Marigold was equally astonished. "It was given to me by the shadow boy. He found it here in Bramblycrumbly under some brambles, but it's really from the Human World—you can see the picture of the humans on the front. But why have *you* been trying to find it?"

Granny hobbled over to the shelves along the wall, where trinkets and all sorts of odds and ends sat. She smiled at the touch of each object. She finally chose a child's stuffed rabbit with part of its ear missing and showed it to Marigold. "This belonged to a girl who woke up on the morning of her ninth birthday with the chicken pox." Granny shook her head and laughed softly as she put it down. She straightened and arranged items on the shelf carefully as she spoke. "There was one child in particular. She was a lonely little girl but full of mischief. I put my wand down for a second and she grabbed it." Granny looked off into space as if she were witnessing it all over again. "It was in the nick of time that she felt bad and gave me back my wand." Granny reached over to the barrel and picked up the Candy Land game. "She also gave me her favorite toy."

"The Candy Land game?" None of it made sense to Marigold. "But how? Did you visit the Human World *too*, Granny?"

Granny gazed at Marigold with a mysterious twinkle

in her eye. Marigold waited for an explanation. The fire burned brightly, and the cottage had the not unpleasant tangy smell of vinegar. All seemed so right—even Boing-Boing purred contentedly in her lap—but no explanation came. "And what about my star, Granny? My parents were so sure that I was marked for greatness— that I was special and would become something rare and wonderful." Marigold searched the old cabbage's face, desperate for an answer.

"You are something rare and wonderful, Marigold," Granny said gently.

"What?" Marigold held out both hands with no idea of what Granny was getting at.

"Don't you know?" Granny said, surprised. "It's right there, child—in the book—or maybe you missed it?"

"Missed it?" Marigold's eyes went wide. How could she have missed it—unless it was missing from the book? The missing pages! Marigold leaped out of the chair and Boing-Boing toppled off her lap. She showed Granny the spell book. "I looked and looked, but there are some pages missing—see?"

"Oh! I am an old cabbage!" Granny exclaimed. She grasped her shawl with one hand while the other loosened the rusty thumb tack that stuck several sheets of yellowing pages to a wooden beam. "Of course you didn't know!" She chuckled and handed the pages to Marigold.

Marigold eagerly read:

MAGIC POWERS can take any number of forms. Here are just a few:

Magic Healing Power

Magic Seeing Power

Magic Hair Styling Power

Magic Large Watermelon Growing Power

Magic Soup Making Power

Magic Finder of Lost Things Power

Magic Friend Power

Wait. What? Marigold stopped. . . . Magic Friend Power? She read the description:

> *Magic Friends (also known as "Imaginary Friends") are extremely rare and have the ability to come to the aid of a friendless human or even non-human residing in the Human World who, for whatever reason, has exhausted all other avenues of companionship. Oddly, Magic Friends usually have little talent for magic—this would seem contra-indicative, but in fact, this feature makes it easier for the Magic Friend to relate better to those in the Human World. . . .*

Marigold looked up from the pages. She had finally discovered her magic power. It all made sense. "No wonder I'm so hopeless at doing spells, Granny!" she exclaimed. "I'm a Magic Friend!"

"Also referred to as an *Imaginary Friend*, child," Granny replied.

"Yes!" Marigold nodded. "I've heard of them but—"

Granny held up a finger to interrupt. "I had the same

magic power as you—I too was an Imaginary Friend when I was your age. Years ago, I tore those pages from the spell book. I kept them here with all my friends' gifts as reminders of what a rare and wonderful magic power I possessed."

Marigold was stunned into silence—mostly because she and the wise old cabbage shared the same magic power, but also because imagining Granny as her own age was utterly impossible. Marigold turned back to the missing pages to read:

> *Magic Friends are usually warned of the friendless in need residing in the Human World through a variety of signals. These signals may be confusing at first, but the Magic Friend soon realizes the meanings of the signals, which can range from a "chirping" or "beeping" sound to a slight pressure on the right pinky toe or even to a blinking star over the head.*

Marigold gasped. *A blinking star?* She had given hers away! How was she going to be a Magic Friend without her star? What had she done? "But, Granny, I lost my magic power when I gave away my star!"

"Roach pudding!" Granny replied firmly, and her eyes flashed in the firelight. She shook her finger at Marigold. "You can't lose your magic power . . . but it will go away if you ignore it, and the best way to do that is to not answer the call."

Marigold and Lightning exchanged puzzled glances. "What call?" they said at the same time.

"When your star blinks, it means someone in the Human World needs you for a friend."

"So, you knew all along when I was here earlier why my star was blinking, Granny. Why didn't you tell me?" Marigold asked.

"Because I knew that you needed to discover your magic power on your own," Granny said softly. "See here." Granny showed Marigold a crayon drawing, a doll in a kimono, and a plastic horse. "These are gifts from some of my friends that they gave me to remember them by. But one gift I lost!"

Granny still held the Candy Land game and offered it to Marigold.

Marigold hesitantly took the game.

Granny grinned. "The little girl who grabbed my wand

wished on it numerous times, and goblins appeared through one of her wishes. I barely completed the Invis-O-Friend Spell.... It was a close call! Upon my return, I landed in Spookety Forest shaken and vowing that I would never let go of my wand—not even for a second—ever again. I ran all the way home, but in my addled state I dropped the game somewhere and was never able to find it—till now!"

Marigold handed the Candy Land game back to Granny, but she wouldn't take it. "When you visit the shadow boy— it will do my heart good to know it's being played with again and enjoyed." Her eyes glistened as she spoke. "I had so many friends—sad ones, sick ones, ones upset over having to go to a new school, naughty ones, angelic ones. . . ." She eased herself back down in her chair and sighed. "But what I didn't expect was that each one had a magic power as well." Granny paused and gazed into the fire as if she were trying to conjure up the faces of all her old friends in the dancing flames. She finally added, "And each one taught me something."

Marigold realized that the same thing had happened to her. Winnie had helped her work the magic wand, Lenny had helped her learn how to fly, and Priscilla had made her realize that she didn't really want to run away from home and live in a shack or even in a little cottage in the woods. Marigold had learned something from all of them . . . except for one: the shadow boy to whom she had given her star.

Granny held up a gnarled finger. "An *Imaginary* Friend—a quite rare . . . and most wonderful magic power."

Marigold shook her head. She sat on the edge of the chair across from the old cabbage. "But, Granny, how can I answer the call of my blinking star if I don't even have one anymore?"

Granny made a dismissive little laugh. "It'll grow back."

"It will?" Marigold whispered. That was a possibility that she had never even considered. She quickly looked up to see if maybe it had started to grow back already. It hadn't.

"At first it will appear like a tiny point of light." Granny held her thumb and her forefinger an eighth of an inch apart. "Then, day by day, it will grow bigger and brighter than it ever was before." Granny raised an eyebrow. "And why is that?"

Marigold didn't answer because she had no idea why.

Granny continued. "Because the more you use your

magic power, the stronger it becomes—never forget that."

Marigold was relieved, but she marveled that she would never have known this if she hadn't given her star away to the shadow boy.

Lightning had been pensive and quiet up till now. Marigold remembered their mutual confusion when he thought she'd been gone only five minutes when she thought she'd been gone a whole day. He must have read her mind because he asked Granny about this now.

Granny nodded like it was a good question. "In those pages there's a section that has 'Rules for Birthdays.'"

"Yes—but it was cut off." Marigold turned to the part in the spell book and read it to Granny. "It says: 'Be advised: It is VERY important that you know there is a—'"

Granny finished the sentence. "'Time difference between Bramblycrumbly and the Human World.'" The old cabbage recited the section, for she knew it by heart. "'Furthermore, Bramblycrumbly will not crumble and turn to brambles unless two conditions are present: a lost or missing wand in the Human World *and* a visible friend who has turned nine years old in the Human World *as well as in* Bramblycrumbly. Since time moves faster in the Human World, it can be years before this occurrence manifests.'"

"There's a time difference—it's the secret twist! Lenny was right!" Not that she had doubted him, but Marigold couldn't help being amazed at the comic book–loving boy's ability to predict that this would happen.

"Whenever you are an Imaginary Friend, Marigold, Lightning will hardly ever miss you . . . unless you have trouble getting back home."

The fire was burning low. Whether it was from a chill or Granny's words, Marigold shivered. "Did you ever have trouble . . . getting back home?"

Granny gave a negative wave of her hand as if she didn't want to talk about it. "That's another story, dear." The old cabbage woman rose and moved heavily toward the door. Marigold gathered up Boing-Boing and reluctantly followed. They stood on the threshold across from each other. "Will I ever get to see Winnie again? Or Lenny? Or Priscilla?" Marigold asked.

"Whenever you want," Granny Cabbage said, but she wouldn't say how. Even though Marigold was curious beyond words, she knew it was useless to press Granny anymore that night.

"It's time for you to go home," she said in a raspy old voice.

Marigold turned to leave and then stopped. "I almost forgot." She had Granny's spell book and handed it to her. "Thank you, Granny."

The old cabbage pushed it back to Marigold and winked. "Keep it. I have a feeling it will come in handy."

16

A SURPRISE FOR BADDIE LONGLEGS

Marigold tucked Granny's spell book into her pocket. She was happy to see that Lightning had gotten over his dislike for the Candy Land game and held it under one arm. As the three set out for home, Marigold wondered how her mother and father would take the news about her magic power, and she braced herself for what they would say about her new human friends. The little houses on Wigglyrambly Way came into view. She spotted the one in the shape of a teapot and landed right in front of it.

Marigold passed through the Dutch door of her house into the kitchen.

"Magic wand . . . make me and Boing-Boing invisible," Marigold ordered.

POOF! She disappeared.

She sidestepped the mashed yam on the floor that her parents had probably hoped one of the brownies would get to overnight. She could smell a fire burning in the living room fireplace. Both her parents sat on the couch watching a wicker basket rock gently in the air. Inside, her sister, Petal, slept peacefully.

"I told you," her father said in a low voice. "The Buoyant Basket Spell works every time."

Her mother kept a keen eye fixed on the basket, like a lion tamer anticipating every switch of the tail of his fiercest cat. "I heard it might rain later—do you think you could activate the Anti-Thunder Spell?"

"Definitely," he replied.

Marigold walked into the room, and the only thing that gave her away was the creak of the wide plank floorboards underfoot, but her parents were too preoccupied to notice. When she was right in front of them, Marigold sat on the coffee table. "Hi, Mom. Hi, Dad."

"Marigold! Is that you?" Her father sounded pleased.

"Magic wand . . . make me visible," Marigold commanded, and she reappeared.

"You did it," her mother whispered, and clapped, barely touching her hands so as not to wake the contents of the wicker basket. But a moment later her joy faded.

Both her parents gasped. "Where is your star?"

"Don't worry, it will grow back," Marigold said cheerfully. "Granny said so."

The orange cat on her lap meowed loudly, and Marigold quickly made Boing-Boing visible too. She picked him up under his arms to show her parents. "This is Boing-Boing."

Of course, both of Marigold's parents wanted to know where in Bramblycrumbly she had suddenly gotten a cat since it had been only a short time since she'd gone off to learn the Invisibility Spell. As far as they knew, she hadn't left her bedroom. And of course, when she told them that Boing-Boing came from her new human friend Priscilla, their shock was nowhere near the level of their distaste.

Her father's beard curled.

Her mother fanned herself as if she might pass out.

Marigold's father sputtered, "You made friends with a HUMAN?"

Marigold scrunched up her nose. "Sort of . . . more than one, actually," she said in a small voice.

Lightning had been staying in the background, but now he sat next to Marigold. The two of them barely fit on the coffee table, but she was glad to have him near for moral support as she told the story of her incredible adventure.

Her parents listened without asking any questions. Marigold saved the most important part, about how she discovered her magic power, for last. "You know how you always thought that I was going to be great at something?"

They nodded because they were too shocked to speak.

Marigold continued. "And you know how I'm only good at being a friend?"

Petal peeked over the side of the basket, which had stopped rocking, and even she listened with rapt attention.

Marigold bit her lip. "And I know you hoped that I'd be a fairy god-doctor or a weather wizard, but as it turns out . . ." She hesitated, afraid of how they would take the news. "I'm a . . . I'm a . . ."

"She's an Imaginary Friend," Lightning answered for her.

Both her parents looked at each other and then at Marigold, and their faces lit up.

"An Imaginary Friend?" her father exclaimed. "Are you sure?"

Marigold nodded several times.

Her father shook his head in disbelief. "Imaginary Friends are very, very rare. . . ."

"How incredibly wondrous!" Her mother gazed at her with pride.

"Why, Bramblycrumbly hasn't had an Imaginary Friend in over a hundred years," her father added.

"Not since Granny Cabbage," Marigold said shyly, but she was amazed and relieved by her parents' reactions.

"ACHOO!" someone sneezed.

All eyes turned to Petal. Her nose was bright red and dripping. Petal screwed up her mouth, squinched up her face, and pointed to her big sister. "Mawigohd no blinky!" she screamed. Then she seemed to notice Boing-Boing. "Achoo! Achoo! Ah-ah-ah-ACHOO! WAAAAAAAAH!"

Marigold, Lightning, and Marigold's mother and father all stood looking at Boing-Boing because they knew he couldn't stay. Boing-Boing was a sorry sight to see. His head drooped. He sniffed, and a tear ran down his furry face and plopped onto the coffee table. It seemed like almost everybody was allergic to him.

Marigold glanced at Lightning, who shrugged. She thought of Priscilla, who loved the cat so dearly and who had so much faith in Marigold to take Boing-Boing.

Her father scratched his head. "Do you know anyone who wants a cat?" he asked.

Petal sneezed several more times.

As a fairy god-doctor, Marigold's mother, Tulip, knew spells for all types of ailments. There were ones for warts, for pains in the neck, crooked toes, even the common cold, and just about anything else you could think of—but there was nothing for allergies except tissues. Tulip twirled her wand, and a box of some appeared. "Maybe one of your friends perhaps needs a pet?" she suggested, and wiped Petal's nose.

"Actually," Marigold said slowly as an idea formed in her mind. "I do know one!"

She hurried Boing-Boing out of the house. She had just thought of the perfect home for him. A moment later she was flying with Lightning huffing and puffing behind her. They passed over Mrs. Moon's, and the owl flapped up from her tree. "I see you've taken my advice and learned to fly with conviction," she said. "But you seem to have a new problem—where's your star?"

Marigold invited Mrs. Moon to follow her where she would tell her all about the incredible adventure she'd been on and how she'd discovered her magic power. The owl followed, curious to hear what had happened.

They passed over Bob the Woodcutter's Son's stacks of wood and saw Bob too. Marigold called to him that she had discovered her magic power and told him to follow her to Baddie's to hear all about it.

On his way, Bob the Woodcutter's Son ran into Marigold's best friends Daisy and Rosie, and Lily and Iris. "Have you heard?" Bob said excitedly. "Marigold Star just discovered her magic power!" Of course, they all wanted to hear her story too. But before Daisy and Rosie and Lily and Iris rushed off for Baddie's, they called the vegetable people Chickpea, Ginger, and Parsnip to tell them that Marigold had discovered her magic power. The vegetable people wanted to hear all about Marigold's incredible adventure. They lived in the middle of Spookety Forest and called Big Flying Bird to fly them to Baddie's. Even Big Flying Bird was curious to hear Marigold's tale and got them there as fast as he could.

"You're back!" Baddie Longlegs shouted, and came running out of his shack as soon as he spotted Marigold. But this time she had a party of all her best friends, the likes of which the solitary troll had never seen under his bridge. Marigold held the big orange cat behind her back.

"I see you've come with some new yarn to surprise me," Baddie said.

"Not this time." Marigold grinned, and Lightning could barely keep from giving the surprise away.

Baddie was puzzled and tossed his head full of beautiful wavy green hair.

"I came to solve your only problem, Baddie," Marigold replied.

Baddie held his hand over his mouth so only Marigold could hear. "But these are all *your* friends. . . ."

"And here is yours for your very own!" Marigold revealed the surprise. "This is Boing-Boing."

"For me?" Baddie took the cat and held him close to his cable-knit sweater. "I've always wanted a cat—I even knitted a bed for one just in case. Want to see it?"

Everyone did want to see, and they were all invited inside to look at the bed that Baddie had knitted in case he ever

got a cat. They weren't disappointed. It was a beautiful shade of buttery yellow, made with special yarn that was the softest in all of Bramblycrumbly. It covered a thick pillow with lovely high sides for a cat to snuggle inside, and as soon as Boing-Boing saw it, he curled up and immediately began to snore. He'd had a long day of it.

Then everyone gathered around to hear Marigold tell the story of her incredible adventure and how she'd discovered her magic power. When she finished her tale with the revelation that she was an Imaginary Friend, no one was surprised.

"We always knew you were marked for greatness," Baddie said proudly.

"But Granny says everyone has a magic power," Marigold replied. "And that you can never lose it unless you ignore it."

This started a lively discussion about what each of her friends thought their magic power was. Of course Baddie's was his extraordinary knitting ability, and Mrs. Moon thought hers was her ability to give expert advice on any subject. When Bob the Woodcutter's Son wondered aloud what his could be, everyone was sure it was his ability to find four-leaf clovers, which were extremely rare, even in Bramblycrumbly. Big Flying Bird was too big to fit inside the shack, but he had popped his head through the window and listened without saying a word, until finally he asked the others tentatively, "Do any of you think . . . ? I—I mean could there be a chance that being big . . . b-big as an elephant . . . could be *my* magic power?" Everyone thought that being big *was* Big Flying Bird's magic power because they all relied on him to carry them through Spookety Forest on a regular basis. The bird puffed up his feathers, which made him bigger than ever, and for the first time he seemed proud of his enormous size. The group talked and talked about magic powers until someone pointed to the top of Marigold's head and shouted, "Look!"

Baddie brought Marigold a mirror, and sure enough, she could see a tiny point of light where her star had once been. "Granny said it would grow back!" Marigold said excitedly. Remarkably, although Baddie hardly ever entertained, he always kept on hand a large blueberry crumble just in case, and he served it now to celebrate. Marigold could have stayed for hours eating crumble and laughing with her friends but not tonight.

"I'll see you tomorrow?" she said to everyone.

Everyone agreed to meet at Baddie and Boing-Boing's the next day. Marigold bent down and kissed the top of the big orange cat's head as he lay sleeping in his new knitted bed. She left happy knowing that Priscilla would approve of his new owner.

Outside, silvery beams of light shimmered from an enormous full moon, and Marigold thought of the one she'd just flown past riding the magic carpet with Winnie. Marigold recited the Flying Spell, and leaped unafraid into the air with perfect timing, just like the superhero that Lenny believed she was. Above, a cloud had formed into the shape of what looked exactly like the shadow boy, and she was reminded that she could never lose her magic power as long as she always answered the call.

Below, the windows twinkled from all the little houses, and strands of smoke curled from their chimneys. Bramblycrumbly had never seemed so magical, and Marigold could have soared through the sky forever with her pet dragon by her side, but they flew straight to 10 Wigglyrambly Way. Tonight, she couldn't wait to get home.

Turn the page for a look at *New York Times* bestselling author Elise Primavera's hilarious, original, and unforgettable novel . . .

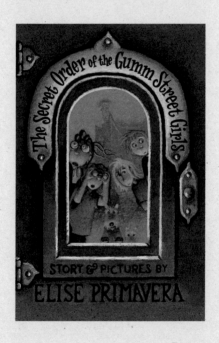

ranny liked the tops of things. She liked mountaintops and rooftops, and she wanted to be at the top of her class and a top-notch cartwheeler. Why? Because in first grade Franny became painfully aware of the middle and the possibility that she might be dismally average.

Franny sighed. Now spring break was almost over and, to take her mind off the horrible reality of going back to school, Franny stood at the top of #3 Gumm Street. Up there, she didn't feel average at all. She felt like Sir Edmund Hillary on the summit of Mount Everest or Amelia Earhart buzzing around in her airplane. Up in her tower she was Fearless Franny Muggs, Queen of All She Surveyed.

She squinted through her binoculars. No sign of Pru. No sign of Cat. *Good*, she thought. She swung around in the opposite direction to have a look at #5 Gumm Street. Not a trace was left from the rogue blizzard that had blown in from the west a few weeks before. It had surprised everyone in town—a blizzard in Sherbet? No one even owned a snow shovel.

One midnight right after that, Franny could have sworn she'd seen lights flickering about inside the old wreck of a house at #5 Gumm Street. She had ducked behind the railing of her balcony and strained her eyes through the glasses to see, but the lights had disappeared. Probably zombies, Franny had decided.

If you believe in zombies (and you should), #5 Gumm Street was the perfect place for them. The house had been vacant for as long as Franny could remember, and vines had taken over to such an extent that from a distance the house looked like a giant hair ball. It leaned so badly to one side that it appeared as if it were caught in a perpetually stiff breeze.

There were no signs of zombies today, though. Instead, Franny spied a moving van off in the distance. It came closer and closer and halted right in front of #5!

Two men hopped out. They carried a few boxes and some ratty old furniture into the house. A moment later a Ford Fiesta pulled up. A woman and a birdlike girl with a bed pillow tucked under her arm—who, Franny figured, was probably the woman's daughter—stepped out of the car.

After a few quick trips, the moving men pulled themselves up into the truck and drove away. The woman and girl went inside through the double front doors that hung precariously from their hinges.

Not five minutes had passed when another moving van arrived. The woman came out of the house, and there was a lot of discussion. The moving men kept pointing and shaking their heads yes, and the woman kept shaking her head no. It seemed like she didn't want whatever it was, and Franny was afraid the moving men were just going to leave—which would be awful, because she was dying to know what was in the truck.

But then the girl came outside and said something to the woman, and she seemed to give in.

With much grunting and groaning, the moving men lifted an enormous, gleaming grand piano from out of the truck and gentled it through the front doors.

Franny went inside at this point. Her tower room was about the size of a large horse stall. There was a small freezer for her Popsicles, a microwave for her hot chocolate, and a desk with a globe on it. Thumbtacked to the small closet door was a calendar with a picture of Mount Everest and a quotation from Amelia Earhart: "Adventure is worthwhile in itself."

New people moving into the zombie house— nothing as exciting as this had ever happened on Gumm Street! *I'll bet there's not even any heat or running water inside that house,* she thought with a thrill. *Maybe in the winter they'll have to melt snow to drink, like Sir Edmund Hillary and his faithful Sherpa, Tenzing Norgay, when they climbed Mount Everest!* It was time to meet the new neighbors face-to-face. Franny hung her binoculars from a hook and clattered down the spiral staircase that wound around and around the outside of her wedding-cake house.

Within moments Franny was on the threshold of #5 Gumm Street. She could hardly wait. She'd always wanted to see what this house was like on the inside. From behind the door came the sound of someone playing the piano. Franny remembered her own piano lesson days. The endless practicing, the interminable scales, topped off at the end of each week by . . . The Lesson. It's true that Mr. Staccato, her piano teacher, was very patient and sympathetic, telling Franny that she wasn't tone-deaf, just "musically challenged." But she got worse instead of better, and once she played so poorly she actually thought Mr. Staccato was going to cry. She stopped taking lessons after that. But what she was listening to now . . . well, it made *her* sound like Beethoven.

Franny knocked.

The music—if you want to call it that—continued, but the door creakily opened, and the woman Franny had seen earlier appeared.

"Hello," Franny said. "My name is Franny Muggs, and I'd like to be the first one to welcome you to Gumm Street!"

"Thanks, hon," replied the woman. "I'm Pearl Diamond, and that's my daughter, Ivy." She hooked her thumb over her shoulder in the general direction of the piano behind her.

Only one word came to mind as soon as Franny saw Pearl Diamond—*sparkly*. She had gleaming blond hair arranged in a complicated way, and on her T-shirt she had rhinestones in the shape of a French poodle. She had sparkly bracelets, sparkly blue eyes, and sparkly white teeth.

"Tell me, hon, you know any piano-type people around here?" Pearl said.

"I'm musically challenged," Franny replied. "At least, that's what Mr.—"

"Staccato," said a man with an English accent from behind Franny.

Franny turned around and there was her former piano teacher, Mr. Staccato himself. He was an older gentleman neatly dressed as always in a three-piece suit. With him were two fat little white dogs, who stood

solemnly on either side of him looking suspiciously up into the face of this new neighbor.

"Miss Muggs," he said with a nod to Franny. "And Mrs. Diamond, I presume. And that must be Miss Diamond"—he politely cleared his throat—"playing the piano."

"Pearl Diamond—you can call me Pearl." Pearl extended her hand, and Mr. Staccato took it by the fingers and made a slight bow.

"Welcome to Gumm Street," he said.

Pearl thanked him, and her hands fluttered self-consciously to her hairdo. "It's the darnedest thing. Someone just delivered a piano, and we have no idea who!"

At this point the music stopped. Franny heard footsteps and

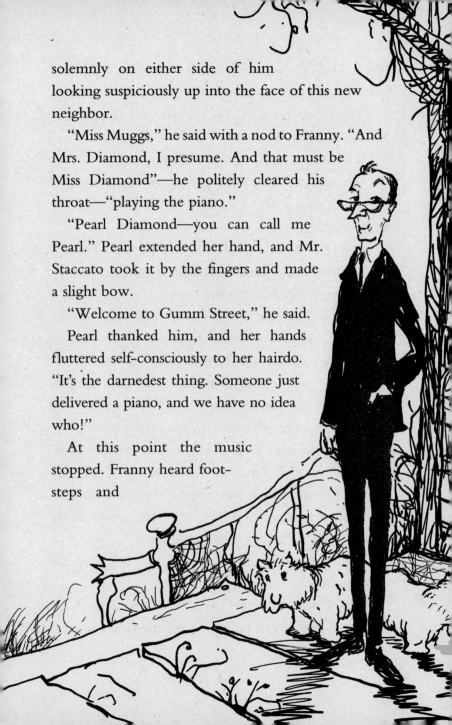

saw the birdlike girl walk over to the door. Pearl put her arm protectively around the girl's thin shoulders.

"This is my daughter, Ivy," Pearl said. "Ivy, this is Franny and Mr. Stiletto—"

"Staccato," Franny corrected her.

"Mr. *Staccato*," Pearl said with an embarrassed little laugh, tucking a stray curl back in her hairdo where it belonged.

"Um, hi." Ivy's eyes darted quickly from Franny to Mr. Staccato to the dogs and finally to her mother, whom she looked at questioningly.

"It must be some mistake—the piano, I mean!" Pearl said, her eyes wide like a game show contestant waiting to see what was behind door number three.

Mr. Staccato leaned forwards, and for a second Franny thought he was going to whisper something in Pearl's ear, like who sent the piano, for instance— which would have been really weird, because how could he know? Then again, he knew Pearl and Ivy's last name, which was weird all by itself. Instead, though, he said in a hushed voice, "My condolences to you both regarding your Aunt Viola."

"Who's Aunt Viola?" Franny said, but everyone ignored her.

"Thank you, but the last time I saw Aunt V, I was Ivy's age." Pearl pulled Ivy a little closer to her.

"We've been on the move the last seven years—kinda had a run of bad luck—but that's all behind us now, right, baby?" Pearl gave Ivy's shoulders a little squeeze, and Ivy smiled weakly, as if she were not quite so optimistic.

"Most interesting," Mr. Staccato mused to himself.

Franny thought that whoever this Aunt Viola lady was, Mr. Staccato sure seemed relieved she wasn't around anymore, because Franny could have sworn he had exactly the same expression on his face as when she had told him she was going to stop taking lessons. She glanced at his two dogs, Fred and Ginger, and they seemed to relax as well. They pulled their tails under, seated themselves, and looked off into the distance, bored.

"Actually, I only met your aunt once, myself," Mr. Staccato said. His face momentarily darkened.

"Then why are you so interested in her?" Franny interrupted, but again the adults acted like they didn't hear her.

"But about the piano," Pearl said, shrugging. "We don't even know how to play this thing!"

"What a coincidence." Mr. Staccato said, and making another little bow, he handed her a card.

"Well, I'll be!" Pearl exclaimed. "If that doesn't beat all."

"That just really beats all!" Franny said cheerfully, trying again to be part of what was going on, whatever it was.

"Doesn't that just beat all, sugar?" Pearl laughed and showed the card to Ivy.

Ivy read out loud, "Mr. Staccato, number seven Gumm Street, Sherbet, piano lessons." She raised her eyes from the card and for the first time looked straight at Mr. Staccato. "You could teach me to play the piano?"

"You never know. . . ." He held Ivy's gaze for a moment while the dogs' ears twitched forwards and back. "You may even have a unique talent for it."

Fred and Ginger jumped to attention. "Good day, ladies." With that, he and his dogs turned on their heels and went briskly down the walk.

"What do you think, baby? Would you like to take piano lessons?"

Franny couldn't believe it when Ivy nodded her head. *Better her than me*, Franny thought.

Noticing Franny once again, Pearl said, "Why don't you girls get to know each other?" Her bracelets jingled as she put on a sequined headband and freshened up her lipstick. "I'm just going to talk to Mr. Staccato again for a moment. Show Franny my Miss Venus Constellation of Stars crown, baby," she called out over her shoulder as she hurried down the steps.

Without a word, Ivy turned and went into the house. Franny followed.

While Ivy rummaged through a few boxes, Franny took the opportunity to steal a look around. It was wonderfully creepy, she thought. The first floor sloped off to the right just like in the fun house at the Sherbet amusement park. In one corner, on the uphill side, was the piano. Its wheels were locked tightly in place and clung to the ancient floor for dear life, so that the piano wouldn't roll and throw the house any more off-kilter. Crooked stairs with some of the banister missing twisted up to the second floor. On the wall halfway up the stairs was a painting of a lady with a bright pink chiffon scarf around her neck and a beehive hairdo. She wore large earrings in the shape of cherries, or strawberries—it was hard to tell in the gloomy light of the house, but clearly they were meant to be some kind of fruit.

"Who's that?" Franny asked Ivy.

Popping her head out of the box for a moment, Ivy said, "Oh, I don't know. Maybe it's Aunt V—Aunt Viola—she's . . . um . . . dead, but she left us this house."

"Oh?" said Franny, climbing the stairs to get a better look. A portrait of Aunt Viola, mysterious and dead, no less, *was* interesting. Maybe Aunt Viola was one of the zombies Franny was sure lived in the house.

But as she got closer, Franny suddenly noticed something: a white envelope wedged in the corner between the painting and the frame. The name *Pearl* was scrawled across it in fancy handwriting.

"Look what I found!" the two girls said at the same time.

Ivy walked over and handed Franny the rhinestone Miss Venus crown.

Franny handed Ivy the white envelope.

"Wow," said Franny. She put the beauty pageant crown on her head and looked around for a mirror. "It's heavy!"

Ivy didn't say anything. She stood biting her lip, frowning at the envelope. She'd never known one not to contain bad news.

"Aren't you going to open it?" Franny asked. She

decided that Ivy Diamond was just about the skinniest kid she'd ever seen, not to mention one of the quietest. She had nice friendly eyes, but her ears poked out through scraggly dirty blond hair, and her narrow face was an unhealthy shade of tapioca pudding.

"It's for my mom," Ivy said, and quickly shoved it into her back pocket.

A second later Pearl came bustling back into the house. "Baby, get ready for some piano lessons!" she said to Ivy. Then she ushered Franny to the door, saying, "You're gonna have to leave now, honey. Ivy's got a lot of practicin' to do, doncha, baby?"

Ivy stood on the porch and watched Franny make her way down the street.

Franny left this first meeting greatly impressed. None of the other mothers were as sparkly as Pearl, and she'd never known a real beauty pageant winner. Franny liked Ivy, too, even if she didn't have much to say. She thought Ivy was pretty brave to live in a house that had a picture of a dead person on the wall (no way would Pru ever do that), and Ivy didn't seem at all stuck-up like Cat.

"Hey, Ivy?" Franny waved and called to her from the street. "Can you do a cartwheel?"

Ivy shook her head no and waved back.

"Good!" said Franny happily. "Neither can I!"